PAULINE TAIT is a multi-gei
in Perthshire, Scotland. After
Technician for just over twenty y
Support, Pauline is now writing
secretly piling up in a drawer for over twenty years, the dust was eventually wiped off her first publication, *The Fairy in the Kettle*, which was published in 2016. The series has since earned Pauline five star reviews.

Married with two grown up children, Pauline is also enjoying writing adult fiction and her novel, *A Life of Their Own*, shows Pauline is not afraid to tackle a difficult subject. With another novel under way and the final instalment to *The Fairy in the Kettle* to come Pauline is looking forward to continuing her writing career.

A Life of Their Own

Pauline Tait

Published in 2019 by SilverWood Books

SilverWood Books Ltd
14 Small Street, Bristol, BS1 1DE, United Kingdom
www.silverwoodbooks.co.uk

ISBN 978-1-78132-915-3 (paperback)
ISBN 978-1-78132-916-0 (ebook)

British Library Cataloguing in Publication Data
A CIP catalogue record for this book is available from the British Library

Page design and typesetting by SilverWood Books
Printed on responsibly sourced paper

Acknowledgements

Many thanks to Helen Hart, Catherine Blom-Smith, Hayley Shepherd and the SilverWood team, my wonderful husband Steven and children, Ross and Rachael.

Also, in one of life's serendipitous moments I would like to thank author, Ryan Lockwood. When I sent an email to the Colorado State Forest Service requesting information on forest management and the local environment, I had no idea the extremely helpful recipient would be a fellow author!

1

Kate allowed herself to indulge in a little apprehensive exhilaration as the changing countryside took her further and further away from her past. Looking down at her two young children asleep beside her Kate knew this was their only chance. Their only chance at freedom and at a life of their own.

The hours were passing slowly, unbearably so at times, and they had seen many other passengers come and go. When they had first boarded the Greyhound bus early that morning in New York it was full, and Kate had watched as it almost emptied again in Philadelphia apart from a few lone travellers. Now though, even they had reached their destinations and, she presumed, were getting on with their lives. Kate and her children, however, still had around thirty-six hours of travelling and many stops ahead of them.

Looking out through the dusty window Kate watched as the bus trundled through the countryside, passing from town to town. She noticed how other women and children were freely going about their business. How they seemed to have a purpose, know where they were going and what they were doing. Some rushing around, jumping in and out of cars, hurrying in and out of stores. Others standing chatting and laughing on the sidewalks and sitting in cafés. It made Kate wonder if she would ever feel in control of her life again, ever find the confidence to make her own decisions. She wondered what her future might hold, whether she would sit in a café again with friends or, more importantly, make friends? She knew she had to. She had to if her and her children's lives were going to be better.

She had told no one they were leaving or where they were going. It was the end of May and the last week of the school term. When she had collected her children from school on Monday afternoon she had told their teachers they would not be in for the rest of that week as they had to attend a family funeral upstate, an excuse she hoped they would never question. School was not back until mid-August, so she would have plenty of time to settle her children in a new home before she had to worry about enrolling them in another school.

They had left the house as normal on Tuesday morning but instead of their usual walk along the tree-lined avenues to school they had posted a letter and boarded the first of many buses. Kate knew that this would only buy her time until Adam, her husband, came home from work that evening, but by then they would have crossed through most of Pennsylvania and be on their way to the Ohio border.

After a short stop in Columbus, Ohio, they travelled through the night, stopping at Indianapolis, Indiana, before arriving in St Louis, Missouri, for breakfast. They had just over an hour to stretch their legs, freshen up and stock up on food and drinks again before re-boarding the bus. Watching the miles roll by for a second day they headed towards Kansas City where they had a one-hour stop for lunch before travelling on to Salina. There they were allowed a short toilet break, before boarding again and travelling on towards Goodland, Kansas, eventually arriving in Denver, Colorado, late that night.

This was their penultimate stop, but it was a long one and the one Kate had dreaded the most. They arrived in the city just before midnight and were not due to get back on a bus again until ten past five the following morning. Not enough time to book into a hotel – not that she'd had much of a chance to investigate hotels. She'd had limited access to a computer to plan their trip and had managed to get most of her information from the lady at the bus kiosk back in New York. Anyway, a hotel room for a few short hours would have been a waste of the money she had fought so hard to gather. Kate knew she had little choice but to settle down in the waiting room of the bus depot with her children.

They were tired, and their bodies ached from sitting so long, but as she encouraged her children to sleep Kate knew she had no option but to stay awake. She was nervous about the time of night and who might be around. An older couple chatted to her for a few minutes, putting her slightly at ease, but this was still going to be a long night.

A television screen was on in the far corner of the waiting room. Her imagination running away with her, Kate watched nervously, terrified her face would appear as a missing person. That was something she hoped she had avoided. The last thing Kate wanted was the authorities looking for her. She had committed no crime other than taking her children away from their father, although most would say that was a blessing if they knew the truth.

The letter she had posted before they boarded their first bus was to Alice Harper, her oldest and dearest friend, and although they hadn't seen each other in well over four years Kate knew Alice would always be there for her. More importantly, Alice knew the truth.

After what seemed like an eternity, the clock ticked round to four forty-five. Waking her tired and confused children Kate gathered their belongings and ushered them for a quick toilet stop before boarding a bus for the last time. Destination: Colorado Springs.

Watching the miles roll by again, Kate thought about how she used to love her life in New York. She had loved her apartment, her job as manager of a fabulously chic clothing store and her circle of friends. She'd had a great sense of humour, impeccable dress sense and enjoyed going out to dinner, to see a movie or a show. She had enjoyed living life to the full and people had enjoyed her company. Now, however, that part of Kate's life was a distant memory. To her, it seemed like a lifetime ago. A lifetime before Adam.

A mutual friend had introduced her to Adam at a party and they had instantly hit it off. They hadn't been together long when Kate found out she was pregnant with their son, Jake. Adam had insisted they get married and for the first few months everything seemed fine, but as time passed Adam developed an incredible jealousy of Kate's bond with her baby. He became controlling and domineering and within a few short months had taken complete control of Kate's life. He hadn't been the most attentive of fathers either and things were only made worse by the birth of their daughter Lucy three years later.

The exact moment that changed the lives of Kate and her children forever was etched in her mind as though it was yesterday. Her boutique had tickets for a New Year's Eve party and Kate and Adam had arrived around the same time as everyone else. They had danced together, laughed with friends and enjoyed the festive celebrations right up to the stroke of midnight. It was while everyone was wishing each other Happy New Year that Adam had been consumed with jealousy. Pete, the boutique's young delivery driver, had innocently kissed Kate on the cheek as he wished her Happy New Year. But the sight of another man showing Kate any kind of affection was far more than Adam could bear, and she could only watch as his temper surged, his face flushing red, hands clenched into fists. Kate could remember trying to push Pete out of the way as Adam lunged towards him, throwing Pete a punch that ricocheted off his left cheek. As Kate's colleagues had gathered round Pete, Adam had grabbed Kate by her arm and dragged her out onto the street. He had pushed her into a taxi and refused to allow her to go back for her coat and bag.

The next working day Adam had phoned the boutique and told them she would not be back. It was her friend Alice Harper who had taken the call. From that moment on, apart from walking her children to and from school, Kate was hardly out of their apartment. Adam wouldn't allow their children to join ballet or soccer or any of the other clubs that their friends enjoyed either, for fear of Kate speaking to any of their fathers.

Adam had always made sure that he provided for them but that was purely to avoid giving Kate a reason to go out. He would go to the supermarket on his way home from work and do any other errands during his lunch break. He took complete control of their finances and gave Kate no form of allowance – another way of ensuring she wouldn't leave their apartment.

She had been a prisoner in her own home until two days ago, when she had left with her children as if taking them to school. She now hoped that in catching one bus after another she had made it impossible for anyone to trace them.

Kate had always liked the sound of life in Colorado: the mountains, the plains, the rivers. Many years ago, she had known someone who had grown up on a ranch outside of Colorado Springs and she remembered how passionately he had spoken about it. She remembered how he had once offered her a life there and especially in recent years she had wondered how different her life would have been if she had been braver all those years ago. Brave enough to give up her life in New York and start a new life with him in Colorado. His name was Matthew, Matthew Harrison, and the last she had heard he was married and living in San Francisco, working as a lawyer. But it meant that in this terrifying attempt for freedom there was a calming familiarity in Colorado Springs.

The grinding of the brakes dragged Kate from her thoughts. At long last the bus was pulling in to their final stop. She had phoned ahead and booked a room in a guest house for two nights. That was all she had allowed herself, two nights. She had spent the last three years trying to gather up as much money as she could without Adam noticing, so two nights would do just now until she could see exactly where they would be staying, make sure it was safe and was worth the money. More importantly, with her very limited budget she needed to find somewhere permanent for them to stay and a job.

Quickly, she gathered their belongings. "Children, wake up. We're here."

Jake and Lucy sat up and, rubbing their eyes, looked out of the window at what was the beginning of their new lives. They didn't possess a suitcase and Kate could only pack the morning they left, just after Adam went to work, so as not to rouse his suspicions. She had quickly put what she could into Jake's and Lucy's school bags and a large shopping bag before telling them it was take-your-favourite-toy-to-school day. So, with the few belongings they had, they struggled off the bus.

Kate could feel her stomach churning. Her heart began to beat faster, and her body was shaking as they left the comfort of the now familiar bus. She looked around; the glow from the early-morning sun was somehow comforting as she looked for a taxi.

"Stay beside me, children," she instructed as she ushered them towards the taxi stand. Pulling a piece of paper from her bag she gave the driver the name of the guest house. "How long will it take?" she enquired eagerly.

"About thirty minutes, it's morning rush hour." The driver looked at them quizzically. She knew why: they were tired and grubby. Their hair was badly in need of a wash and the usually smart mother and children looked like they hadn't eaten properly in a few days. Which was true – they had left New York early on Tuesday morning and it was now early on Thursday morning.

Piling into the back of the taxi Jake and Lucy snuggled into their mother. She knew it was a lot to put her two young children through but their trust in her was absolute and they followed her instructions without question.

Staring out of yet another window they sat quietly as their driver jostled with the traffic. Their guest house was in a suburb on the outskirts of Colorado Springs. Although Downtown looked bustling and appealing Kate wanted to be near the countryside. The fact that it was also much cheaper was a welcome bonus. She wanted her children to breathe the fresh mountain air. They had spent far too long cooped up in their New York apartment leaving only to go to school.

As the taxi slowed to a halt Kate looked out at the traditional house sitting in a quaint but tidy garden. After paying the driver and stepping from the taxi Kate was aware she was standing still, staring at the house in front of her. She could hear the taxi drive off behind them and a wave of numbness spread through her body. She had done it. She could not go back. She could not go anywhere other than into the house that stood in front of her. She knew no one, knew where nothing was, not the schools, the shops, the doctors. A scary and isolating feeling for a mother with two young children who was used to her husband making all the decisions.

Decision one, however, was to go inside…

2

A woman in her mid-seventies with a round kindly face opened the door. Her wispy grey hair was pulled back and rolled into a bun at the nape of her neck. She wore an apron over her smart floral dress and a light cardigan that looked as though she may have knitted it herself.

Nervously Kate introduced herself and her children.

"Welcome, welcome, come on in," said the older lady, standing back and taking a good look at them over the rim of her glasses. "I'm guessing that if you are arriving at this hour of the morning you are all in need of a good hearty breakfast?"

Jake and Lucy looked up at their mother. They'd had more than enough of bus depot food in the last fifty hours and the thought of a decent breakfast was putting a smile back on her children's faces.

"That would be lovely."

Kate and the children followed the old lady down the hallway and into a room at the back of the house. A round table was already set for three.

"This is the dining room. I will show you everything else once you have eaten but for now enjoy the view." She gestured towards the large window at the rear of the room.

Kate sat as her gaze rose from the roofline, over a thick line of trees and up to the Colorado mountains she had so desperately needed to be close to. The mountains she had been dreaming of for so long were now right in front of her. She could feel her eyes filling up but checked herself and turned to tend to her children. She pulled their tousled hair back from their faces and smiled at them. "Once we've had our breakfast we will get cleaned up and changed into our other clothes. If you would like we could maybe find out about going into town for some supplies this afternoon?"

Her children smiled and nodded.

"Here we go," the old lady said chirpily as she came back into the dining room holding a large wooden tray. "I thought perhaps some homemade pancakes with bacon and maple syrup might be a nice treat for today. There is also bread, cereal and fruit on the sideboard so tuck in and help yourselves."

The children's faces lit up. "We love pancakes!" Jake exclaimed, looking up at the old lady as Lucy's arms shot out to grab her pancakes.

"I'm very glad to hear it," she replied, returning a few moments later with a pot of much-needed coffee for Kate and milk for the children. "My name is Maggie, Maggie McAllister. If you need anything else just give me a shout – I'll be in the kitchen."

Kate watched her children as they sat silently but happily eating their food. It wasn't an awkward silence, it was a calm and relaxed silence which Kate thought was odd given their circumstances. But Maggie had put them at ease instantly. She had asked no questions about where they had come from, why they looked so bedraggled or why they had so little luggage.

When Kate had phoned ahead to book the room it was from a pay phone she passed each day as she walked her children to and from school. Each day she had looked at it knowing she was one day closer to putting her plan into action. When the day had finally come for her to make the call she was trembling so much she could hardly speak. The telephone had been answered by a kindly voice.

"Speak up, dear, you are very quiet," the voice had requested on more than one occasion.

Kate had only given her first name. When asked for a surname Kate had replied, "It's just Kate."

She had gone on to explain that her children were eight and five and that they had no choice but to arrive early because of the bus times and wondered if they could possibly have breakfast upon arrival?

Maggie had been left wondering about the mysterious lady on the other end of the phone. She and her husband, Walter, had run the guest house for almost thirty years. They'd had all sorts of people come and go and Maggie had become good at reading people's characters and situations. She had spotted the East Coast accent in Kate's voice when she had phoned and had presumed a long journey was involved. Then adding the two young children into the mix and the fact they weren't staying with family or friends, Maggie knew there had to be more to it. Especially when they turned up looking so bedraggled and with virtually no luggage. She knew that although it was none of her business a little mothering wouldn't go amiss.

It wasn't long before the pancakes were polished off and two milky moustaches were arched over two little smiles. Kate could feel the coffee kicking in and after wiping her children's faces they got up to look for Maggie. They found her leaning over a large rectangular table in the centre of the kitchen. She was cutting shapes from cookie dough, much to Jake and Lucy's delight. Looking up with her usual beaming smile Maggie wiped her hands on her apron. "Come on then, let me show you around."

Maggie took them back out into the hallway which ran through the centre of the house. There were two large living rooms. Both were homely with plain cream walls, floral sofas and cushions. Both had a television in the corner, open fireplaces and drapes to the floor. One had a low table in the centre with a selection of games, playing cards and colouring sets, while the other had a vast selection of books and an old-style record player in the corner with a collection of albums to choose from. From there Maggie took them back up the hallway. The dining room, where they had eaten their breakfast, was off to the left and opposite it was a door to the downstairs toilet. A further door at the end of the hallway took them through to an L-shaped kitchen. The kitchen led to a rear extension where Walter and Maggie had their own private living quarters.

They followed Maggie upstairs. There was a bathroom and three double bedrooms, each with a small shower room. Maggie showed Kate into the larger back bedroom. As well as a double bed there was room for a pop-up single bed which Maggie had already put in place, and most importantly to Kate, it had views out to the mountains.

"Now, is there anything else I can help you with, dear, before I leave you all in peace?"

Kate turned to face Maggie, a wave of panic suddenly rising inside her. "We all need showers. Our clothes are badly in need of a wash as we don't have very much with us at all. We need to go into town to buy more clothes and toiletries, but I have no idea where town is. I need to find a job and we need to find somewhere permanent to stay."

Kate was taken aback. She had blurted the words out so quickly she hadn't been able to stop herself. She stood quietly, her cheeks flushed, wondering what to do next.

"Well, my dear, don't worry about a thing," Maggie said softly, clearly unfazed by Kate's outburst. "You have plenty of time. My husband, Walter, is out running a few errands for me just now, but he'll be back soon with groceries and a copy of the local paper. You can have a look in the job section later. This afternoon, once you and the children have showered and had a chance to rest, Walter can run us all into town. I can point you in the direction of the shops you need. As far as finding somewhere permanent to stay, my dear, I know children sharing and a pop-up bed isn't ideal but the room you are in is available for as long as you need it. Walter and I are getting older so we just let out one or two rooms at a time now, usually just to regulars. It helps with the pension and we enjoy the company. Oh, and if you leave your dirty clothes outside your door I'll come back up in a while and collect them, get them going through the machine before we head into town. How does that sound, dear?" Maggie gave Kate a warm smile of reassurance.

Kate just smiled back, at a loss for words and still embarrassed at her outburst, but Maggie could see the panic fading and the appreciation in Kate's eyes. Maggie hadn't taken charge the way Adam did but in a few short minutes she had offered Kate solutions that allowed her to do what she needed to do in this strange environment. The act of kindness was unusual and gave Kate a strange sense of calm. She had chosen the guest house because it was not part of a chain and didn't appear to be highly advertised. But she was now realising that was only because its owners weren't promoting it; they had a trickle of regular customers and that was enough for them at this stage in their lives.

"I can ask around about jobs too. I'm guessing something that works around school times would be good?" Maggie asked as she headed out the door.

"Thank you," was all Kate could manage as Maggie's

words spun in her head. School. She knew that was something she was going to have to deal with, but not now, not today. One thing at a time.

As they climbed into the back of Walter's black truck Kate began to panic. If she bought the clothes that she and her children needed she would be spending money that she couldn't afford to spend. She thought she had enough saved to see them through for four or five months, but only if she found a job, and she couldn't start a job until her children were in school. And which school? Which neighbourhood would be best for them, best for a school? How would she know? Her head began to spin, the way it always did when she felt things were spiralling out of control. She turned to look at her two smiling children. They were asking Walter all sorts of questions about his truck.

"How high is it?"

"Can we sit in the front?"

"Can it go through water?"

"Can we get one?"

Their questions were much simpler, less terrifying. She had decisions to make but not today. She would buy them a few new pieces each to keep them going a while but what they needed most of all was a good night's sleep.

"Welcome to Colorado Springs shopping mall!" Maggie exclaimed with a chuckle as she climbed down from the parked truck. "Shops are that way," she signalled, pointing towards a door at the far end of the car park. "You will find everything you need in the mall. Perhaps start on the upper floor and work your way down. How long would you like, dear – we could meet back here in two hours, or longer if you need it?"

"Two hours would be perfect, thank you, Maggie," Kate replied gratefully. "And thank you, Walter."

Kate made her way through the mall, Jake's hand on one side and Lucy's on the other. She felt exposed, unsure of what to do. She hadn't shopped or even wandered round a mall in years and she had forgotten what it was like. Her thoughts drifted to Adam, resenting him for depriving them of such a simple pleasure.

"Look, Mum!" Lucy shouted, pointing to a pair of jeans and a t-shirt in a shop window.

"Do you like those?"

Lucy nodded.

"Come on then, let's have a look." Kate led her children into the store and slowly they looked around. There was a wide variety of clothes for both Lucy and Jake and the prices were not too bad either.

"Okay, pick two pairs of jeans, one pair of shorts, three t-shirts and a fleece each and then we will go and try them on."

Fifteen minutes later Jake and Lucy were stood in front of her with their arms laden. She laughed as she ushered them towards the changing rooms. Jake went into one by himself while Kate went into the one next door to help Lucy. "Let me see each thing as you try them on, Jake," she shouted back through the adjoining wall.

Twenty minutes later, her children were stood in front

of her again with smiling faces and clothes that fit. She took them over to the underwear section, and to get pyjamas, and once they had been added to their pile they went to pay.

"Right," said Kate as they left the store. "Now we have to find clothes for me."

She walked from window to window, taking it all in. Glamorous clothes intermingled with classy casuals adorned the mannequins, beautiful bags draped over their arms and jewellery to finish. She couldn't afford anything like that. She looked down, but her mournful look didn't last long. Her children were beaming, happy to be free although they didn't realise they hadn't been. They hadn't strolled through a mall like this in years – in fact Lucy never had – and they were taking to it like ducks to water.

As they rounded a corner, there in front of them was a store Kate recognised from the years before. They wandered inside. She found a couple of pairs of jeans, a pair of dress pants in case of interviews and three tops that could be dressed up or down, a fleece and some new underwear. She quickly searched for a scarf, her secret from the past for dressing an outfit up when needed. After trying everything on she paid, and they headed off again. Now shoes for Kate and sneakers for the children. They each needed a spare pair as they only had the sneakers they had travelled in. They found a store, not the best quality but the price was right for now, and it wasn't long before they are walking out again, with another bag to carry, and heading towards a drug store for toiletries.

*

"Finished and with half an hour to spare," Kate said, smiling at her children. "Who would like ice cream?"

"Me!" chirped the two little voices in unison.

They wandered round to an ice-cream store Kate had spotted earlier. Jake and Lucy looked at the vast array of flavours and after making their decisions they headed out into the warm Colorado sunshine to enjoy their ice cream. A chocolate-chip cookie dough, a choco mint and a cookies and cream were all going down a treat, and that is exactly what it was, a treat.

Ice creams done and faces wiped, it was time to head back to the truck.

3

The mail arrived at 8.05am, just as Alice was leaving for work. She picked it up as she did every morning and threw it on the sideboard to open later – after all, who had time to open their mail in the morning? Picking up her bag and heading towards the door, she stopped, glancing back at the larger envelope in the pile. She recognised the handwriting. It was handwriting she had been looking at every day for the last four years. Kate was not only one of Alice's dearest friends, she had also been her boss. When Adam had phoned the boutique to say Kate would not be back Alice had been promoted and was now the manager. The files and notes in her office that preceded her were all in Kate's handwriting.

Picking up the envelope she sat on the edge of her sofa, feeling uneasy. Alice hadn't heard from Kate in just over four years and she knew it wasn't because Kate didn't want to speak to her. It was because Adam wouldn't allow it.

Tall, blonde and always impeccably dressed, Alice gave off a quiet air of confidence. She was smart, took no nonsense and she knew Adam found her intimidating. Although if she was honest she would have to admit that she encouraged that as a way of keeping him at a distance. Alice had never trusted him, and he knew it. Adam had, therefore, gone out of his way to make it impossible for Kate and Alice to spend any time together. But Alice was intelligent, and she knew Kate better than anyone. They had been the best of friends and although unspoken, Alice knew exactly what Kate was going through. She had seen Adam in action and was sure things had to be much worse behind closed doors. While they had worked together, she had often told Kate that she would be there if she ever needed her.

Slowly Alice opened the envelope. Inside she found a letter addressed to herself and two smaller envelopes. She read her letter, trying to make sense of what Kate was telling her but also what she was being asked to do.

The two smaller envelopes were to be delivered by Alice personally: one to Adam and one to Mrs Jamieson, Jake's school teacher. Kate knew her request was unfair on Alice, but she couldn't risk Adam coming home to a letter the day they left. She needed to buy her and her children as much time as possible. Nor could she risk Adam receiving a letter with a post mark. If she posted a letter in New York, he would presume they were still living there and, although that would centralise his focus, it would also mean he would never give up and that was a thought that filled her with dread.

For the same reasons she couldn't risk a postmark on the letter to the school. She had no idea if Adam would contact them, but she needed to be sure she left no hint as to their whereabouts; it was the only way she could be confident of starting over. At the same time, mailing it on their way to Colorado Springs was also far too much of a risk, that would give Adam a glimpse into their route.

The last thing Kate wanted was the authorities looking for her. Her children were not missing. She was not a missing person. She was someone who had finally taken control of her and her children's lives.

Adam had a temper, but he had never stooped so low as to harm his children physically. It had always been verbally: loud, controlling, manipulative and belittling. With Kate, however, it had also been physical, and because she had not stood up to him at the start Kate felt she was somewhat to blame...that she had allowed it to continue. She would tell herself that wasn't the case, that it was Adam's problem and there was something wrong with him. But the truth was she wasn't brave enough to stand up to him, to stand up to his vicious temper. She had always stayed quiet and let him have his way in the hope that things would quieten down much more quickly.

Alice knew that Adam would have had two days of torment, and two days of not knowing where his wife and children were would have driven his temper to new heights. She also knew that he would not have gone to the police for fear of his actions being found out. Adam loved them in his own, albeit unhealthy, way but Alice knew Adam well enough to know he was aware his actions were wrong. It was his own fears and insecurities that had caused him to behave the way he did. Deep down he would know he had driven Kate away.

Okay, first things first, Alice thought to herself, Kate and the kids are free and that's the most important thing.

She phoned the boutique and explained that something had come up and she would be in sometime before lunch. She wasn't due on the shop floor this morning anyway; this morning was admin and it could wait. She took a deep breath as she picked up the phone and dialled the old number she had for Kate, hoping it was still live. The ringing lasted a mere second as a frantic-sounding Adam answered the phone.

"Kate!" he shouted, the rage in his tone evident.

"No, it's Alice."

"What the hell do you want? I've told you before Kate doesn't want to talk to you. Now fuck off and don't call here again."

Alice shuddered at the ferociousness of his tone and gripped the receiver harder as if it would give her the strength to keep talking. "I've had a letter from Kate in the post this morning and there's one here for you too. Meet me at Benito's Coffee House in forty minutes."

Alice hung up. She wasn't going to give Adam the chance to start any nonsense with her. She picked up her bag and once again she headed out the door.

Benito's Coffee House was always bustling so she knew

Adam would have to keep his temper in check. She wasn't going to give him the chance to speak to her; she was going to say what she had to and that would be that.

Nonetheless, Alice waited nervously. Bloody hell, she repeated to herself, as her heart threatened to beat its way right out of her chest. She didn't take her eyes off the door. Adam was ten minutes early, as she had expected. When he walked in his face was scarlet. Alice could tell he was only just managing to suppress his temper. She knew he would hate not being in control of the situation.

"My letter asked only that I give you this. I know nothing else. I don't know where they are," she stated quickly but firmly as she handed him the letter and left.

She walked as fast as she could towards the busiest end of the street, almost bursting into a run. Her heart was pounding in her chest and beating in her ears.

"Please don't follow me, please don't follow me," she repeated under her breath as she hailed a taxi and jumped in.

Slumping into the back seat she gave a sigh of relief, not daring to look back. She had no idea if he had chased her to ask her more questions or if he had stayed in the café to read the letter. The last thing she wanted was Adam thinking she was a link between him and Kate. He would never leave her alone and she didn't want anything to do with him.

Coming back to her senses, Alice looked at her watch. It was just after nine. She probably wouldn't be able to speak to Jake's teacher until classes stopped for morning break, but she knew she would be better getting across town now.

"*Where to,* miss?!" The taxi driver sounded impatient and Alice realised he'd been repeating himself while she sat lost in thought. "If you're not going to tell me where you want to go you can get out."

"Sorry, sorry, I need to go to..." Pulling the other letter from her bag Alice pointed to the address.

Not another word was said between them until the driver pulled up thirty minutes later outside the school.

"Would you wait please?"

Sensing that Alice wasn't exactly having the best of days, the driver nodded. Shutting the door behind her Alice ran up the steps to the school entrance and pressed the buzzer.

"Hello," a voice crackled through the intercom.

"Hello, I need to speak to Mrs Jamieson urgently. Is it possible to speak to her now or can I come back sometime this morning?"

"Are you a parent?"

"No, my name is Alice Harper and I'm a friend of Jake and Lucy Thomas's mum."

Suddenly there was a buzzing sound and the door was unlocked. Alice signalled five minutes to the taxi driver and went inside.

Walking up to the reception Alice was met by a bubbly lady in her fifties. Just the type to welcome you into a school, Alice thought to herself.

"Mrs Jamieson is with her class, but I have just sent someone along to relieve her and she will be with you shortly. Please take a seat."

The receptionist signalled towards a row of grey chairs nestled neatly against a pale blue wall. Very clinical, Alice thought as she took a seat.

A few minutes later a tall, slim, dark-haired lady walked down the corridor towards her.

"Hello, I'm Mrs Jamieson, please come with me." Alice followed her into a little office adjacent to the reception. "Please take a seat."

Alice sat down again and took the envelope out of her bag. She handed it over and sat quietly as it was read. Alice had no idea what the letter said so she was unsure as to whether she would be needed for anything else.

Kate had written to Jake's teacher because she knew she had an idea of what life had been like for her and her children at home. Mrs Jamieson had tried to broach the subject on several occasions, suggesting that it might be good for Jake and Lucy if they met with their friends socially out of school or joined an after-school club. But Kate would never be drawn. She had been far too scared, and Mrs Jamieson had sensed her apprehension. Now, however, Kate needed to explain everything.

Kate's letter started by thanking her for being somewhat aware of their situation and for doing her best to make her children as involved with their fellow classmates as she possibly could. Kate knew that Mrs Jamieson had discussed her thoughts with Lucy's teacher often, and that they had been keeping an unofficial eye on the family situation. However, both teachers had known they were good, well-cared-for children who had everything they needed. They'd had no concerns other than socially but had worried about how their isolated environment might impact on their futures. They had noticed how the smiles on Jake's and Lucy's faces would vanish if they were given an invitation to a birthday party or asked if they wanted to go to a friend's house for a play date. The children knew the answer would always be no. Mrs Jamieson was also aware that the children were only ever in school or at home, but Kate's letter went on to reveal exactly what life had been like for her children and how their father's behaviour had impacted on them. Mrs Jamieson did know, however, that the children were happy – after all, they had known no different.

Kate also explained a little of what life had been like for her and why she had needed to get them away. She explained that she would be enrolling her children into a school as soon as they were settled and in time for the August start, so their education would continue uninterrupted. Kate wanted to make sure that she was not in any trouble with the authorities.

Alice had done her bit. She thanked Mrs Jamieson for seeing her at such short notice and left before running down the steps and into the waiting taxi.

"This is going to cost you," the driver quipped.

"I know, but it was worth it," Alice replied, and she gave the driver the address to her work.

As Alice settled down in her office to catch up on admin her thoughts kept drifting back to Kate and her children. Kate's letter had said only that they were no longer in New York – there was no mention of where they had gone. The thought of not seeing Kate again was painful but Alice was also relieved she didn't know where they were. Adam couldn't get information out of her if she didn't have it to give and she was grateful to Kate for that.

4

Kate opened her eyes. The sunlight was streaming in through a small gap in the curtains and as she sat up she couldn't help but smile. She knew that whatever they did today was up to her. Making her own decisions was taking quite a bit of getting used to. She found that constantly having the confidence to know she was making the right decision was hard but as each day passed she felt a little stronger and, very slowly, she felt her confidence was starting to return.

Getting out of bed she glanced over at her two beautiful children, still sound asleep. Lucy was a miniature Kate. Her eyes, her colouring, her hair was all Kate, and she often saw herself in Lucy's expressions. Jake on the other hand was a mix of both his parents. He had his father's sandy blonde hair and hazel eyes, but he too had Kate's facial expressions, so

Kate was never reminded of Adam when she looked at him.

It wasn't quite time to enrol Jake and Lucy in school and there was still plenty they wanted to do. They had become far more active in Colorado Springs, regularly walking into town, playing in the park or going for ice cream. Jake and Lucy often helped Walter in the garden and kept him company on his errands. They especially loved packing their backpacks, jumping into Walter's truck and heading off for walks through the forests. Jake and Lucy loved being amongst the trees. They loved how they looked so majestic here in Colorado, so different from the organised tree-lined avenues they were used to in New York. They loved the height and stature of the Douglas Fir and Ponderosa Pines and would quite happily sit against them looking up into their canopy as they ate the lunch their mother and Maggie had packed for them. They could easily spend a whole day amongst the trees, wandering, looking, listening. The call of the birds was like nothing they had ever heard in New York and the scuttling sounds on the ground would send Jake's and Lucy's imaginations into overdrive as they tried to decide what creatures were lurking around.

Kate could see her children becoming more sociable and it filled her heart with joy; after all, she had done this for them too.

Sitting down at her dressing table she looked at herself in the mirror. She brushed her hair and drew her fingers across her face. She was only thirty-four but recently she had felt about a hundred.

Not bad I suppose, she thought to herself as she pulled at the skin around her dark brown eyes. She examined the ends of her hair and could only sigh. Her hair had not been cut in months. Adam had given her money for her last few appointments but she had kept it, putting it towards her savings for their escape. She had told him that she had decided to grow it and had just had a trim to take the very ends off. He hadn't noticed any different.

Kate was completely unaware of her beauty and although she couldn't afford to keep up to date with the latest trends she had a tall, slim build and a timeless natural beauty, an elegance. People noticed her. This had been lost to her though as her own self-confidence had disappeared in recent years.

She decided she would talk to Maggie and ask her to recommend a salon; Jake and Lucy could do with a trim too. Maybe some make-up, she thought, something natural but enough to make her feel human again.

This had to be a positive sign, Kate realised. She was starting to think about herself again.

Stepping into the shower she thought about what the day would hold. She couldn't look for a job until her children were in school, but she had been doing errands for Maggie, cooking, ironing and a bit of housework, and in return Maggie had been knocking a bit off the rent. She was spending less money keeping a roof over their heads than she had budgeted for, which had allowed her to treat herself and her children to a few more pieces of clothing.

The prospect of looking for a job once Jake and Lucy

were in school excited her. She worried about finding something that would fit around school, but she knew a job would be good for her, that it would give her a purpose and help her meet new people. What she was going to do during school holidays was a worry though. She didn't think she would be able to afford both rent and childcare and the thought of having to take time off work unpaid also worried her.

Stepping out of the shower she quickly dried herself and got dressed. The guest house was homely, and she felt safe there, but privacy was virtually impossible. She looked over at her children still sound asleep in the double bed. She had spent the last few weeks on the pop-up bed and although comfortable enough, spreading out in a double bed would be nice. She didn't want to blow-dry her hair for fear of waking her children from their sleep, so she brushed her long brown wavy hair and left it to dry. It was going to be another frizzy day, she thought as she let out a sigh.

Every now and again she would allow herself to think about looking for somewhere more permanent to stay. They were needing their own space, their own beds, rooms if possible, and to be surrounded by their own belongings – not that they had many of those. She would have to look for a small house or apartment to rent. Something furnished to start with and maybe somewhere close to Maggie and Walter. They didn't realise it, but they had become surrogate parents and grandparents to Kate and her children and they were very fond of them. She suspected the feelings were mutual.

The sound of her children stirring brought her from her thoughts.

"Good morning, sweethearts. Did you sleep well?" They murmured sleepily that they had, rubbing their eyes as they took in the new day. "Okay, well, we've got books to return to the library this morning, so how about you get yourselves washed and dressed and have some breakfast, and after the library we can go to the park and onto the diner for some ice cream."

The promise of the park and ice cream was enough to get her children moving and before long, the three of them were dressed and sitting down in the dining room eating breakfast.

After helping Maggie to wash up, Kate and her children left the guest house and headed towards the library. Kate politely said good morning as she passed neighbours. She was beginning to recognise people and, although she desperately wanted her own place, she had a sense of belonging here that she was finding comforting and relaxing.

As they reached the steps of the library Kate watched her children run up them two at a time. She felt their newfound sense of freedom and enthusiasm was both saddening and inspiring at the same time. While Kate went to return the borrowed books Jake and Lucy went off in search of new ones. Her children could quite happily spend hours in a library and this pleased her. After thanking the lady, Kate too went to look for something new to read. Although this time she was looking for something different, not the usual novels she had been borrowing.

Kate scanned the shelves, pulling a book out, reading the blurb and putting it back. She did this repeatedly until one took her interest: *Starting Your Own Business on a Budget*. This might do, she thought.

Her quiet unspoken panic at being a single mother in a town where she didn't know anyone was always brewing somewhere just below the surface. She was toying with the idea of running her own business from home. The managerial and paperwork side of it would be easy – after all she had done it all before in the boutique – and although the income wouldn't be great to start with she hoped she could work it around a part-time job until she got going.

While she had been stuck in her apartment day after day in New York Kate had spent a lot of her time baking. Although not her passion, it helped pass the time and was something she was good at. She used to hand some into neighbours if there was too much and after a while some started to put in requests. Just enough that she could bake during the day and deliver without Adam knowing. She soon realised that if she kept some of the baking each day for themselves she could justify the need for the ingredients to Adam while at the same time charging her neighbours a small fee. Small enough to encourage them to ask her again but as she was secretly stashing it away it had built up and helped towards funding their escape.

Eventually, they had gathered up a selection of books between them. Taking them up to the counter Kate handed over the library card to be scanned. It was in Maggie's name. Kate had not yet given her surname to anyone, not even to

Maggie or Walter. She knew she would have to at some point but not yet. Not until she had found somewhere to stay and was enrolling the children in school. Adam was almost two thousand miles away, but she had no idea if he had reported them missing, if people were looking for them, or worse, if he was looking for them. She felt the fewer places their names were registered the better.

As they left the library Kate picked up a local real estate guide. It was time she started looking, at least, getting a feel for what was available and, more importantly, an idea of rental costs.

They walked through the beautiful Colorado sunshine towards the park. The view of the mountains rose up in the distance and it was a view Kate loved. Finding a bench Kate settled down and keeping one eye on her children she had a quick scan of the guide. It didn't take her long to realise that the rental costs for the type of property she was looking for would make life very tight financially. The deposit alone would take a big chunk out of what money she had left. She knew she could stay at the guest house for as long as she needed but she also knew she and her children needed a home of their own.

Her mood had taken a dip. She didn't know what to do for the best. She looked up at her children playing happily. Jake was at the top of the climbing frame, as usual, and Lucy was on a swing. Kate tried to bring them to the park three or four times a week. There was always other children and Jake and Lucy were now starting to mingle with them. Kate hoped that when they did start school there would be some familiar faces from the park and maybe she would get to know a mum or two.

Today was quiet though. There were two boys about Jake's age, but they were there with what looked to be their grandmother, and an older girl that Lucy was chatting to appeared to be there alone. It was going to be much harder for Kate to make friends.

Soon the sunshine brought her two thirsty children. Time for ice cream. A short walk away was an old-style American diner which had become a favourite for both Kate and her children. The long narrow diner had booth-style tables down one side that looked out to the street and a counter that ran most of the length of the opposite side. The décor was red, white and silver and the staff were always welcoming. They were starting to become familiar with Kate and her children, which was nice, and the ice cream was delicious!

They chose a table quite far from the door, and a content silence fell over the table as Jake and Lucy tucked into their much-anticipated ice cream. Kate sipped at her coffee and had another look through the real estate guide, just to see if moving slightly further out of town would make a difference to the rental costs.

There were small apartments which she thought she might manage to afford but nothing with a garden, and the children loved running around at Maggie and Walter's. Kate had also enjoyed being able to sit out with a book once her children were in bed. It was a luxury they hadn't had in New York, but it made a huge difference here and she was hoping to find something with even a small garden if she could. Using the marker pens she withdrew from her bag, she scored out in black anything that was no good. Anything she marked with a red dot, although a financial stretch, could be a possibility. Any properties she found that sat comfortably within her budget were either completely run-down or just one bedroom with a sofa bed in the living room. She had hoped for three bedrooms, two at a push. The children could share for a little while longer.

She read through from page to page, area to area. She was still trying to familiarise herself with the different locations in Colorado Springs, and when she glanced up to ask a passing waitress about an address she noticed a tall dark-haired man entering the diner. It was only from the side, but she felt as though her heart had stopped beating. She watched his profile change as he turned and walked up the centre of the diner towards them. She could feel her face flush with panic. He stopped at the counter and Kate managed to catch herself enough to drop her head. It was him!

"Good morning, Matthew, what can I get you today?"

"Usual coffee to go, thanks, Tina."

Shit, Kate thought to herself, he can't see me like this. Not today, not with air-dried hair and no make-up on. Her head began to spin the way it always did when she panicked. He must be passing through. He can't live here, he's a lawyer in San Francisco. He must be visiting his dad. But what if he lives here? What if our paths have crossed and he's seen me before, but I've changed so much that he didn't recognise me? Her head had gone into overdrive.

She had thought about him often. He was her biggest regret. The one she had let slip away.

Coming out of her thoughts she sat with her face half hidden behind her hand. Hidden enough so that she could still see out and watch him from the corner of her eye but he couldn't see her. She watched him as he waited for his coffee, paid then turned to go. As he walked towards the door her heart began to race. She watched as he opened the door but turned back to chat to an elderly couple sitting just inside. Kate absorbed every inch of him. He was dressed in blue denim jeans and a navy and grey checked shirt, tucked in, sleeves rolled up to just below the elbow. His mud-clad boots made her wonder if he was back at his family's ranch. He was looking more muscled than she remembered, a little older but he suited it – and that smile! That bloody smile hadn't changed a bit.

She watched as he said goodbye and walked out the door. Her eyes followed him as he crossed the road and stepped into a blue Ford pickup and drove off.

Kate sat quietly. She looked at her children, who were almost at the bottom of their ice creams, and started to wonder if she had dreamt the last ten minutes. It was too much of a coincidence. He looked like Matthew, the waitress had called him Matthew. She thought about asking the waitress just to be sure, but she worried she might tell him. Not that he would have any idea who the woman with the much longer than usual frizzy hair and two young children was.

Kate folded up her real estate guide – there was no concentrating on that now – and sipped at the last of her coffee. Her children's chatter brought her from her thoughts.

"Right, come on then," she said, trying to sound cheerful. "We had better get these library books to the guest house."

They gathered up their books and walked across to the counter to settle their bill. The waitress was having her usual chat with Jake and Lucy, asking if they had enjoyed their ice cream, when Kate was suddenly aware of a figure standing over them. She turned to see Matthew. He was as tall and dashing as she remembered and was looking straight into her eyes.

"I know you didn't want me to see you, but I couldn't—" he broke off. "I couldn't just drive off as if you weren't here. I couldn't. Why hide, Kate, why would you hide from *me*?"

Kate could only look at him as tears began to flow uncontrollably down her cheeks.

"Are you alright, Mum?" Jake asked, grabbing her by the arm.

Kate smiled down at him. "Yes, Jake, this is an old friend and it's nice to see him."

"So, it's those funny happy tears?"

"Yes," Kate nodded, hiding the truth. The truth that she wanted to run into his arms and have him hold her forever. The truth that she had never stopped loving him. The truth that he was now married to another woman and working in San Francisco.

"We need to talk," Matthew pleaded.

Kate was suddenly aware that the four of them were walking towards the park. Jake and Lucy were delighted to be having their second visit in less than an hour, and ran to the climbing frame as Kate and Matthew sat on the same bench she had perched on earlier.

He was the first person she had met in months that she knew, and he was someone she could trust completely, someone she could be open and honest with, and that felt good. She had kept so much to herself for so long and it felt good to finally talk without caution.

They quickly fell back into their old relaxed rhythm and chatted like they had never been apart. Kate found herself pouring her heart out. Her words kept flowing as the strain of the last few weeks and years was vented in minutes. She told him everything. Well almost everything; she stopped short at the most painful part. The part she felt sure she would never be able to talk about to anyone, especially Matthew.

Matthew put his arms around her and pulled her close. His body felt strong against hers and her heart and head wrestled with each other as she found it comforting and arousing and all too confusing. After what felt like an eternity, she lifted her head.

"What about you, are you on holiday? Are you visiting your dad?" she asked, hoping the answer was yes. It would be far too hard to stay in Colorado Springs if he was married and living here, right under her nose. She couldn't bear the thought of bumping into him regularly, especially if his wife was with him.

"No, I've moved back,"

Shit, she thought. I can't stay here now, I just can't.

"I'm divorced. I came back to help Dad run the ranch."

"Divorced?" she repeated, almost needing confirmation.

"Yes, divorced, four years ago. It would seem I'm a country boy at heart! You will have to come over to the ranch and see Dad some time, he would love to see you."

"I-I don't know," she stuttered.

Bugger, she thought to herself. This morning she had felt settled, that she was starting to belong and had a plan. It was a vague plan, but a plan nonetheless. This had just thrown everything up in the air.

She watched her children – they were happy here too. She had just under two weeks before she had to enrol them in school and everything had been coming together nicely. But now what was she going to do? She needed simplicity, to be in control of her life without any heartbreaking distractions. She had no idea if Matthew had thought about her over the years the way she had of him. Was she a closed chapter in his life and he was just happy to see her, nothing more? She needed to think. She needed to get away from him, from his eyes, from his comforting arms and from that bloody smile. She had to clear her head. She had to decide if she and her children could stay in Colorado Springs with him living so close by. Kate knew Matthew was not part of her life anymore, but she also knew she couldn't settle into a life here where she could bump into him at any moment.

She wouldn't tell Matthew where she was staying but she did take his number. Not that she'd had a choice, as he wrote it down and insisted she take it.

Matthew could sense Kate's confusion. He knew he had

complicated things by turning up in her life and he could see that her marriage had had a huge effect on her, but surely she had to be glad to see him. Surely she still had some feelings for him. He found it hard to see her so broken and worn out by life. He wanted to run back to New York and give Adam what he deserved but he could also see a flicker of the old Kate. He felt she wasn't too far under the surface and that maybe she just needed time to work out what had just happened and how she felt about him.

Matthew stood up and leaned over. He kissed her on the forehead and whispered, "I have always loved you, Kate. You have my number – use it when you're ready." He walked over to Jake and Lucy to say goodbye. They were still giggling at the sight of him kissing their mother's forehead but smiled at Matthew as he turned and left. No one saw the tears brimming in his eyes as he walked back towards his truck.

5

Turning into the entrance of Wester Lakes Ranch, Matthew looked up to the mountains, just as he always did. Although this time with the same broken-hearted feeling he'd had the last time he had seen Kate, when he left New York for good and returned to the ranch alone. He was frustrated. All those years ago a life almost two thousand miles away was far too terrifying for her and yet now this was where she had run to escape and build a new life for herself and her children. He could understand why. It was a big world out there and he understood the familiarity – it was a place she had heard so much about – but he also knew that it wasn't going to be easy living and working here with Kate living just a few miles away.

The long driveway took him through land that had been in his father's family for four generations. The lush grassy fields were fed by nutrients that came down from the mountains, giving his family rich fertile grazing land before it gave way to the drier plains.

Matthew brought his truck to a stop outside the ranch house which sat in front of the forest at the foot of the mountains. Behind it were three bunkhouses and to the left a large outbuilding. The road carried on past two further outbuildings before curving round to the left toward the pastures where the stables and cattle sheds stood. The road, which was by then a dirt track at best, meandered through their land, criss-crossing the river that wound its way from the mountains above them down through their land and on towards Colorado Springs. The track eventually stopped outside three further bunkhouses. Although they were now unoccupied they had glorious views looking back across the fields to the ranch house and the mountains behind.

Matthew had grown up at Wester Lakes and it was in his blood. His mother had died when he was too young to remember, and Emma, their housekeeper, had become like a surrogate to him. She had made sure he got to and from school on time, was in clean clothes and took him to soccer and basketball practice. She had made sure he did his homework on time and had friends round to visit. John, Matthew's father, had been able to save the ranch through tough times because Emma was there but that hadn't taken away from the relationship he had with his son. John always made sure he saw Matthew before he went to school in the morning and that they spent time together each evening after dinner. Emma, her husband Jesse, their two children and the ranch hands had been Matthew's family.

As Matthew got older his love of the ranch and the land was evident and he became a paid hand. His father, however, had insisted he go off to study another profession and get a degree. John had known that the life of a rancher went up and down depending on the economy and the seasons and he had come close to losing the ranch once or twice himself in the early years. He had wanted to ensure that if Matthew took over the ranch he had something else to fall back on, unlike him. Ranching was all John had ever known but fortunately he was competent at looking after the books, budgeting and forecasting, and the ranch had flourished.

Reluctantly, Matthew had gone to New York to study law. At the time he thought it would be a good career with good money, but the collar-and-tie lifestyle and built-up city life proved not to be for him.

It was while studying law that he had met Kate. She was a year above him at university and studying business. She had been sitting across the table from him in the library one afternoon and Matthew couldn't take his eyes off her. It had taken him a few days to muster up the courage to speak to her but once he had they became very close and dated for three years. When Matthew graduated Kate was already working and had just become manager of the boutique in the city. Although Matthew had graduated, he was without a job and was heading back home to the family ranch, a prospect all too scary for Kate.

Jesse and Emma had worked for Matthew's family for almost forty years. Married and in their late fifties Jesse was lead ranch hand and had Matthew and his father's complete trust, while Emma was housekeeper. She was kind, gentle and known for running the house like clockwork and feeding the young ranch hands as though they were her own children.

As machinery had advanced over the years the number of men needed on the ranch had decreased. When all the bunkhouses were full twenty-four ranch hands had lived and worked at Wester Lakes. Jesse and Emma had lived in the first of the three bunkhouses behind the ranch house since they were eighteen. It was their home, and after all their years of service John had promised it would remain so, rent-free, once they retired.

The other two bunkhouses could house up to four ranch hands each. The second was home to the three youngest hands. Dylan, nineteen, was learning the ropes under the watchful eye of Jesse, while Cody and Jason, twenty-five and twenty-six respectively, had both worked on the ranch since they were eighteen.

The third bunkhouse was home to Owen, twenty-nine, who had a real skill when it came to the livestock. It wasn't unusual for Sarah, his girlfriend from Colorado Springs, to spend the night either. She never got past Emma and was always dragged in for a hearty breakfast before she left to catch her bus to work. Now she was part of the wider group and no one thought anything of it.

Blake, Jesse's right-hand man, shared the third bunkhouse

with Owen and the occasional Sarah. Blake was a real asset to the ranch; he knew all there was to know about breeding cattle and horses and had taken Owen under his wing. He could see he had real potential and a love for the animals.

Divorced and in his early forties, Blake had come to Colorado six years ago for a fresh start. He had used his savings to buy a small plot of land a few miles up from Wester Lakes and was slowly building a house for himself. He was building it in stages, one phase at a time, as he saved. Now though, it was structurally sound, the electrics and plumbing had been installed and the kitchen was partially fitted. The next stage would be completing the kitchen and installing the bathrooms before finally starting on the decoration. His aim was to be moved in within the next twelve to eighteen months and be mortgage-free. This excited Owen as he was quietly hoping that when Blake moved out Sarah would move in.

Wester Lakes was like a family, working in harmony with one another most of the time, and in a beautiful part of the country.

Matthew sat quietly on the veranda. It was mid-afternoon, and he had plenty he should be getting on with, but all he could think about was Kate. He was in love with her. He always had been, and his feelings today were as deep as the last time he had seen her. He knew he wasn't going to sit back and let her go again but he also knew he had to go about things in the right way. He just wasn't sure what the right way was or even how he was going to find her again.

Matthew knew that although it was a word Kate had

never used, she had been abused. Abused by her husband for years – the evidence was there to see in Kate; he had seen it for himself today. He could tell she felt alone and vulnerable. Vulnerable yet determined, he thought to himself as he leaned back in his chair. He knew determination showed strength. Maybe given time this could be the start of something better for all of them.

6

Kate was still rooted to the spot on her park bench. She hadn't wanted to go back to the guest house as she knew her eyes were still swollen from her tears and she couldn't get Matthew's parting words out of her head. *I have always loved you.*

Her head was spinning. After all these years could they both be feeling the same way? He was obviously ready to move on but seeing him today had only reinforced to Kate how broken she was. She had always tried to avoid thinking about herself, thinking about what she had been through, always putting her focus on her children. It was self-preservation. Nonetheless Kate was all too aware of the damage Adam had done to her both physically and emotionally.

A few other children were starting to arrive at the park. Any other time Kate would have been delighted. She would have watched to see if Jake and Lucy connected with anyone, maybe even tried to strike up a conversation with another mother. But not today. Today she was a mess and would be mortified if anyone spoke to her. So, standing up she quickly gathered the library books she had been carrying around all morning and called on her children.

Kate watched Jake and Lucy as they walked slowly back to the guest house. They had colour from all their time in the sun and were looking healthier. She knew they were happier than they had ever been, and she was proud of how effortlessly they had settled into their new life here in Colorado Springs. She also knew that moving them on again could undo the good that had been done, and there was also Maggie and Walter. Staying close by would be good for all of them, and anyway the thought of starting over was making her stomach churn.

Jake and Lucy ran up the path to the guest house and opened the front door.

"Hi, Maggie!" they shouted in unison.

"Oh, hello, children, you are just in time – I'm about to start lunch," Maggie replied from the kitchen.

Kate watched as Jake and Lucy ran up the hallway but didn't follow; instead she went upstairs to her room. She looked at herself in the mirror, at her frizzy air-dried hair and her red puffy eyes. She barely recognised herself. Seeing Matthew and thinking about the past so vividly had brought back memories of the person she used to be; the young twenty-something with her whole life ahead of her. She searched her reflection desperately hoping for a glimpse of her former self but all she could see was a mess. A mess both inside and out!

She was brought from her thoughts by a knock on the half-open door.

"I'm making coffee, dear. Would you like a cup?" Maggie asked, poking her head round the door, but before Kate could answer Maggie was striding towards her. "Oh, Kate, what's the matter?" she asked, putting her hand on Kate's arm.

Kate burst into tears again. She brought her cupped hands up to her face and sobbed into them uncontrollably.

"Here, here sit down." Maggie pulled Kate down to sit on the edge of the bed, and put her arm round Kate's shoulders. "It's alright, dear, let it out. It's always best to let it all out."

They sat, with Kate sobbing uncontrollably, for what felt like an eternity. Suddenly Kate stood up. "The children, they can't see me like this," she blurted.

"It's alright, they're helping Walter out in the yard."

Kate sat back down again. "I'm a mess, Maggie, and I have to do something about it, but I don't know where to start."

"Well I'm here if you need me, dear, you know that."

"I know, but it's hard to talk about." Especially as Kate didn't want to talk about it. She didn't want anyone here knowing what she or her children had been through. Matthew was different, he was Matthew. Kate started to sob again.

"Look, dear, you don't have to tell me anything, but maybe if I tell you what I know it might help us to find a way for you to move forward."

Kate lifted her head and looked at Maggie. Whatever did she mean? What could she know?

"You have been here for just over two months now. There has been no mail, no telephone calls, no visitors and when you arrived you knew not a soul here. You are supporting yourself and your children alone and you have never told us your last name. You arrived here with nothing – you hadn't even packed properly. People staying here for a week arrive with far more than you did. So, I am guessing you had no choice but to leave and leave quickly. This is a much-needed fresh start for all of you."

Kate could only stare at Maggie. Her swollen eyes had widened; she was speechless. Kate had never considered what Maggie and Walter might think about them. They had welcomed them into their home on a much more permanent basis than they normally would, and Kate was only now beginning to fully appreciate that Maggie had known what she was doing all along. Maggie and Walter had shown them nothing but warm hearts and kindness from the minute they had walked through the door and that had had a big part to play in the ease with which they had settled into their new life in Colorado Springs.

Kate decided she was going to have to tell Maggie a little about her life. There was no way she was going to speak about her past but maybe Maggie could help her with the here and now. Taking a deep breath, she took the old lady's hand. "No one knows we're here. We had to cut ourselves off from everyone we knew so that we could be sure of starting over. We haven't done anything wrong – we aren't running from the police or anything, but we couldn't stay. Not with the life we had.

So, we boarded many buses and came here, to the Colorado mountains." She gave a half-hearted smile as she glanced out the window. "I have no idea if anyone is looking for us, which is why I've never told anyone our last name. I know I'll have to when the children start school, but I'll cross that bridge when I come to it."

Maggie gripped Kate's hand. She had tears welling in her eyes too. She had welcomed this lovely family into her home and a kinder mother and nicer children she could not have met. The thought that they had been through something so terrible and had no option but to run the way they had was breaking her heart.

"I met someone today, Maggie. Someone I knew years ago, before I was married. Someone I loved very much, and I know he felt the same way about me. I thought he was in San Francisco, but he came into the diner near the park today. I know I can't move the children again. I know we must stay here, but it's unsettling. I don't think I could bear living here knowing I could bump into him at any moment. This morning I knew what I was doing, but now…"

"Do you care about this man, the man you met today?" Maggie asked softly.

"Yes, and he's divorced, but I can't think like that. I'm a mess and—" Kate broke off again.

"Kate, you came here looking for a new life, a fresh start. You had no idea what that life would be like, but you had a vision of what you hoped it would be. That vision was a fantasy built in your head to give you the strength to carry out what you had to in order to get here, to where you are today. Now though, now you are faced with many choices. This is the time where you must open your eyes to all that is in front of you, the reality of life here in Colorado Springs for you and your children, and decide how you want to take your lives forward. Don't let your past stop you from grabbing what is here for you now if it's what you really want."

Kate sat deep in thought. "I loved him, Maggie, I loved him with all my heart, but I loved my husband too at one point and look where that got me." Kate thought for a moment about how she had inadvertently fallen into a life of misery. There had been no warning signs that she could remember, nothing to make her think Adam would be anything other than... Kate paused mid thought. Suddenly it struck her with a blow all too heart breaking and yet all too honest. She'd had no reason to think he would be anything other than *like Matthew*! Kate was now realising Adam was her rebound guy, the guy she had fallen for quickly after Matthew had left. He had filled a void, distracted her from her heart break, and she had gone into the relationship with both eyes closed.

Maggie drew her from her thoughts. "Do you believe that the person you met today could be anything like your husband? I think not. I think that if you thought he was you wouldn't even be entertaining the slightest notion of him being in your lives. Perhaps you're afraid because you care deeply for this man, and you are scared you are no longer the person you used to be."

"He's nothing like my husband, Maggie, nothing, I know that, but..."

"But you feel that life has changed you and you can't be sure that things would work out anyway? None of us have a crystal ball, Kate, but we must have faith in our choices. I'm guessing you made a bad one years ago but that has been followed by many good ones. Look at where you are now and look at Jake and Lucy. You have raised two very happy and well-mannered children." Maggie's voice was stern but kind. "You're far more capable and intelligent than you give yourself credit for, Kate."

Kate knew exactly what Maggie was doing. She was giving her a gentle but much-needed kick up the backside. Maggie was right: Kate had to decide what she wanted from life, what she wanted for her future and for her children's future, and she had to start by sorting herself out. She gave Maggie a hug. "I don't know what I would have done without you and Walter, I really don't."

"I have no doubt you would have managed just fine, dear, but we are glad you came here, to us. Now let me go and get you that coffee," Maggie said with a smile.

"Oh, and a suggestion for a hair salon?" Kate asked, tugging at her frizzy hair. "First things first, I have to deal with this mess."

7

Kate and Maggie chatted as she and her children headed to the hair salon. Maggie had a few errands to run and had offered to walk into town with them. The sun was shining, and the deep blue Colorado sky always had a way of lifting Kate's spirits.

"Here we are, dear." Maggie gestured to the large smoked-glass window up ahead.

Kate was a little surprised. The salon was trendier and a bit more upmarket than she thought Maggie would usually go for, but then she wondered if Maggie had chosen this one especially for her. Kate had just presumed she was going to the same salon Maggie used. They said their goodbyes and Kate and her children went inside.

Maggie turned around quickly and walked back in the direction they had come. She was saying hello to people she knew but was desperate not to meet anyone she knew well. She had no time to stop and chat today. So, keeping her head down she took a shortcut and headed towards the park.

Ten minutes later she was crossing the street from the park to the diner. It had been a while since Maggie was last in and it had been refurbished. Everything was clean and bright, and she could see why Kate and the children liked it so much. She hurried up the central aisle and waited as a young couple settled their bill. It was Tina behind the counter, which was good as Maggie had known her mother for years. When the young couple had finished paying Maggie stepped forward. She had no idea if she was doing the right thing, but no one had to know.

"Good morning, Maggie, I haven't seen you in a while. How are you?"

"I'm fine, dear, and you?"

There were a few minutes of pleasantries, how's your mother and that sort of thing, but Maggie knew she had to get to her point.

"Listen, dear, you know the young lady staying with me – she has two young children, Jake and Lucy?"

"Oh yes, those two definitely love their ice cream," Tina chuckled.

"Yes, yes they do," Maggie replied quickly. "Well they were in here the other day and a man spoke to them. They knew him from years ago. He is apparently from around here. Any idea who he was?"

Tina looked puzzled. She knew Maggie was a kind-hearted soul who would have a good reason for asking.

"Strictly between us, Tina, I promise," Maggie prompted.

Tina leaned in and lowered her voice. "It was Matthew Harrison from Wester Lakes."

Maggie could feel the smile spreading across her face. Matthew Harrison, oh yes, she thought to herself. He would do nicely.

"Thank you, Tina, thank you. Say hello to your mother for me, dear." And with that, Maggie strode out the diner like a woman on a mission.

Maggie busied about finishing her errands but couldn't keep the smile off her face. Matthew Harrison of all people, she thought to herself. She had known him when he was a young boy, had often met him in town with Emma, but she hadn't seen him in years. Walter knew his dad quite well, had helped him out with a few odd jobs over the years. She was going to have to sit quietly on this one until she worked out what she was going to do next.

But instead of walking up the front path to her house Maggie walked up the side and had a look to see if Walter's truck was there. It was. She wasn't too keen on driving it. Far too big, she would say, but if she took it out for a run in the country she wouldn't have to worry about parking or driving through the heavy traffic. She glanced back at the truck again. Needs must, she thought as she headed towards the kitchen to make a start on lunch. Putting some eggs on to boil she grabbed the bread. Walter heard her and came to help. They chatted about their morning, but Maggie didn't mention her visit to the diner.

"I need the truck for a while this afternoon," she announced out of the blue.

Walter looked at her, open-mouthed. She was more than welcome to the truck, but Walter knew she hated driving it.

"What for, dear?"

"I need to run an errand but it's a surprise."

"Uh-oh, okay, well, I promised old Mr Lynch I'd help him with his fence this afternoon. You could drop me there and then leave me the truck when you're done."

Perfect, thought Maggie. Before long, they had prepared a large plate of delicious egg mayonnaise sandwiches. Maggie was just taking them through to the dining room when Kate and the children returned.

"Just in time," Maggie announced, smiling.

Jake and Lucy rushed to give her a hug, as was standard on their return these days.

"Well look at you two, very smart," she said, admiring their haircuts. "Come on, lunch is ready."

Jake and Lucy sat either side of Walter, smiling and chatting to him while they eagerly awaited their lunch. Kate went into the kitchen to see if Maggie needed any help.

Kate had had a few inches cut from her tired, dry hair and it was now shiny and full of body. Her naturally wavy hair was sitting about three inches below her shoulders and framed her face perfectly.

"Ah, beautiful, my dear!" Maggie's expression couldn't hide her delight.

"I needed a few inches taken off and I've had my make-up

done too while I waited for the children to get their hair cut. I even bought some. It's been quite the treat!" Kate said, laughing, as the two women joined the others for lunch.

An hour and a half later and Maggie was leaving Colorado Springs. She drove towards the mountains and marvelled at the scenery as the dry plains gave way to shrubs and grasses, the lush green forest looming ever closer. It was a road Maggie knew well, a road she had travelled many times when she was much younger. A few miles on past Wester Lakes Ranch was The Lodge. It was a family-run hotel and restaurant now but when Maggie was young The Lodge was the place to go for a good night out and some dancing. She'd met Walter there, although she'd had her eye on him for a good while beforehand. Good choice, she thought to herself, smiling as she drove on towards the mountains. Walter had been as solid as a rock during their years together and she couldn't have been happier. Children would have finished things off nicely, but it wasn't to be, and they had come to terms with that. Maggie often wondered if that was why they had opened their home up to others for all these years.

Soon Maggie found herself turning into Wester Lakes. She followed the driveway as it cut through the countryside and came to a stop outside the ranch house. Looking around she spied a young ranch hand tinkering under the hood of another truck. The young hand was Cody and he looked up to see who was there. The large truck made Maggie look even smaller and the sight of such a small elderly lady clambering out of it made Cody chuckle.

"Can I help you?" he called over to Maggie.

"I'm looking for Matthew, is he here?"

"He's over at the cattle sheds." Cody nodded towards the buildings in the distance. "Vet's out paying a visit today so he's down there keeping an eye on things."

Maggie looked at the road ahead. She could see there wasn't much of it left before it turned into a dirt track. She glanced back at the truck. Cody must have sensed her apprehension because the next thing she knew he was offering to drive her round. He closed the hood of his truck and nodded to Maggie to jump in.

It was a good five-minute drive round to the cattle sheds and by the time they got there Maggie had discovered she knew Cody's grandparents well.

"I'd better behave then," he joked, bringing the truck to a stop. "Matthew's in there – if you give me a minute I'll go get him."

Climbing out of the truck slowly Maggie tried to take in the surroundings. It was beautiful, peaceful and so close to the mountains she felt she could almost touch them. A few minutes later a tall, handsome man came striding out from one of the sheds. His dark hair was tousled, and he had mud splattered on his face. He was wearing dark blue overalls tucked into mucky boots. She began to wonder if she was doing the right thing. She felt she may have come at a bad time and didn't want to be an inconvenience.

"Good afternoon, I'm Matthew." His strong, kind voice instantly put Maggie at ease.

"Hello, Matthew, my name is Maggie, Maggie McAllister. You might remember me from years ago?"

Matthew vaguely recognised the elderly lady standing in front of him as a friend of Emma's from years back but was polite in his response. "Of course, Maggie. How are you?"

Maggie stiffened as if trying to reinforce the courage that had brought her to the ranch in the first place.

"I'm fine, thank you. I-I wanted to let you know that Kate and the children are staying with me. I just wanted to make sure you knew that, that's all," Maggie stuttered nervously.

"With you." Matthew took a step closer. Maggie noticed instantly the affection in his eyes when she mentioned Kate's name.

"Yes." She handed Matthew a small piece of paper. "That's our address and telephone number should you ever decide you need it. I don't want to interfere, but I felt—" Maggie broke off. She knew she had either done something wonderful or terrible but right at this moment she had no idea which. Matthew leaned back against the truck, his hands falling to his sides.

"I saw her the other day."

"I know."

"She was Kate, my Kate from years ago. She was still in there. I haven't been able to stop thinking about her since, but I think I made things worse. I confused her. She has been through so much."

Maggie put a hand out to silence Matthew. "I don't know what happened to Kate in New York. She hasn't told me. She only told me about you. Well actually she doesn't know I know who you are, she only told me about a man from her past, but I found out who you were."

"How?"

Maggie looked down at her feet. She was an honest person and being deceitful didn't come naturally to her at all. "I'd rather not say. But please know I'm here because I want what's best for Kate. She and the children have become like family to Walter and me, and Kate needs to heal, but before she can do that properly she has to move on. She needs to decide what route to take and make a new life for herself and her children. What's concerning me is the route she chooses. I'm worried she chooses what she sees as the only safe route, but it might also be the loneliest." She looked up at Matthew and smiled nervously. "I will say to you what I've said to Kate – follow your heart, dear. Now it's up to you two. Now, I should go – I'm driving Walter's bloody great big truck and I'd rather get that over with."

Matthew laughed and shouted for Cody. "Thank you, Maggie. I'll be in touch soon. I just have to figure out what to do next."

Maggie smiled to herself as she climbed back into Cody's truck, relieved that she'd had the courage to do what she'd just done.

8

The time had come for Kate to enrol her children in school, a moment she had been dreading since she first stepped foot on the bus in New York. She knew she would have to come clean about some of their past to ensure their safety in the future, but it was not going to be easy. She presumed that the normal procedure would be to have files forwarded on from their old school, but she didn't want anyone knowing where they were.

Jake and Lucy held onto their mother's hands as they walked through the school gates. School didn't start until tomorrow, but they were being shown round today and Kate would have to fill out their enrolment forms.

They walked up the steps and Jake pressed the buzzer. A lady looked out from an office window and pressed the button to release the door and let them in.

The school was much smaller than the one they had attended in New York but it was bright and cheerful, and Kate hoped that was a good sign. As they entered, they could see a long corridor with classrooms to the left and offices and a reception area to the right. Kate told her children to have a seat while she went to speak to the lady behind the desk.

Her stomach churning, Kate looked at the extremely young lady holding the enrolment forms. She didn't look to be more than twenty-two, twenty-three, if that. I can't talk to such a young girl about what we've been through, Kate thought. I can't, I just can't.

She glanced across to a much older lady sitting behind a computer, wishing she could speak to her instead, but it seemed the young twenty-something was on desk duty.

"Good morning! This must be Jake and Lucy?" The cheerful voice and bright smile didn't put Kate at ease at all and she struggled to get words to come out of her mouth. The receptionist looked at Kate slightly oddly. She obviously wasn't sure what was happening, but she tried to politely gloss over the situation and kept talking.

"These are the enrolment forms. If you take a seat you can complete them just now and once you're done Mr Saunders will give you a tour around our school."

"I...I would rather complete the forms after I've spoken to Mr Saunders."

"He's showing another family around the school just now, it was just to save you time, but you are more than welcome to wait."

Kate nodded and turned to sit down beside her children. Mortified at her own inability to speak, she wondered what the young lady was thinking. She didn't dare think about it any longer.

Jake and Lucy were looking up at a wall strewn with photographs. Soccer, hockey and basketball teams were lined up holding various cups and awards from over the years as well as individuals who had excelled in athletics.

"Would you like to join some of the clubs?" she asked, looking at them both optimistically.

"I don't know," Lucy replied. She was nervous, and Kate knew she would have to take things slowly with her.

"What about you, Jake?"

"Maybe soccer, but I don't know the rules very well. Dad never played it with me."

Kate felt sick. It was almost three months since they had left New York, and Jake had never once mentioned his father. Was it good or bad that he had chosen to do it today? She had no idea. Was the prospect of starting a new school bringing home to Jake the reality of their new life? Her mind went into overdrive and her head started to spin the way it always did when she was panicking. She had to calm herself and calm herself quickly. She couldn't meet the principal like this.

Happy thoughts, happy thoughts, she kept telling herself repeatedly. Come on, Kate, happy thoughts, happy thoughts. Before she knew it, she was thinking about Matthew standing in the diner talking to the elderly couple at the door. She was thinking about his tall stature, his muscled arms and, there it was again, that smile. An overwhelming sense of calm spread across her.

It took her by surprise but the more she thought about it, he was her happy thoughts. Apart from her children, her only other happy memories were with Matthew and the boutique before he left to come home. She thought about how happy they had both been when she got her job there. Kate had loved clothes, but she loved bookkeeping, admin and organising more. She was a great organiser. Funny how she had forgotten that. She had completely turned the boutique around, increasing its sales by fifty-four percent in her first six months.

How could she have put all of that so far back in her mind that it was only now coming out, like it was news to her?

Suddenly she was dragged from her thoughts by the sound of voices coming from the corridor. She looked round to see a tall, slim man in a grey suit and a family beside him: a mother, father and two children that looked to be possibly around the same age as her own. They chatted at the door for a few minutes before the tall man in the suit opened the door and walked them out. Very pleasant goodbyes were heard before he returned. Smiling at Kate and the children, he went to speak to the young receptionist. When he turned around to approach Kate his expression had changed to one of intrigue. Bugger, she thought, this is it.

"I believe you would like a word before I show you around our school?" he asked politely.

"Y-yes please," Kate stammered. She turned to Jake and

Lucy and instructed them to stay right where they were before following Mr Saunders into his office. He walked behind his desk and gestured to Kate to take a seat. He was mid-forties, she thought, maybe fifty and well dressed. He appeared efficient and authoritative but kind too.

Kate looked towards him nervously. "I'm not sure where to start." She could sense his concern. The poor man had no idea what she was about to say but he was not pressuring her to get on with it.

He simply said, "Well sometimes it is best to start where you feel most comfortable and we'll go from there."

Kate was only in his office for twenty-five minutes but it felt more like hours. In that time she explained what life for her children had been like in New York and how Adam had treated them. That her children had excelled academically but that they had no experiences socially with anyone other than herself and Adam until they came here. She told him about their journey to Colorado Springs, how she felt they had settled in here and how they had flourished over the last three months. She made sure he was aware of the lengths she had gone to ensuring they were untraceable, which led her to her next question, the one that scared her the most. How could she enrol her children in school, give their full names and ensure they could never be traced?

Mr Saunders sat back in his chair. He had let Kate speak, not interrupting her once. He knew it was best to leave her to her flow, that way nothing vital would be left out, but he had made notes in his pad as he listened. He looked at her, at her appearance and her demeanour. He had met parents of all types over the years and he felt Kate's story was genuine. He was, however, aware there were always two sides to every story and he had to remain impartial. He could only comment from the school's point of view.

"Firstly, let me assure you that the staff here will do whatever they can to help Jake and Lucy settle in and I will also monitor their progress. Secondly, as far as giving their full names, there is no way around that. We do usually make attempts to get pupils' files from previous schools, but I can ask that that be delayed indefinitely for now. However, if I feel there is a need further down the line I will ask for them."

Kate had not named their previous school, but she knew it would only take a casual chat between a teacher and one of her children and it would be out there.

"As far as your husband or last school finding out, you have crossed state lines and are now out of the New York jurisdiction. Your previous school won't show on any of our systems and this school won't show on any of the New York systems, unless we tell them you are here to allow them closure."

Kate sat forward in her chair. She looked directly into Mr Saunders' eyes for the first time since she had sat down. "You have my word that we will fully integrate and respect the school. You have my word that my children will arrive on time and work hard, and I will support the school in every way I can. But if there is any hint that my husband has found out where we are we will be gone, without a trace. I will protect my children from him, Mr Saunders, for as long as I live."

Kate could feel the tears welling in her eyes and tried to compose herself. Leaning forward in his chair Mr Saunders smiled, and she knew at that point she had him on side.

"Come on, let's start our tour." He stood and ushered Kate towards the door.

Jake and Lucy were sitting right where she had left them. She knew they would be and that the receptionist would have been keeping an eye, but they were happy to see her.

During their tour, Kate couldn't be happier with what she was seeing, and Jake and Lucy were all smiles too. They both met their teachers: Jake would be with Miss Simons and Lucy with Mrs Walker. Both were mid-thirties, and both seemed friendly and approachable, which pleased Kate.

After the tour they followed Mr Saunders back to reception and the young receptionist came forward again with the enrolment forms in her hands.

"Mrs…er…sorry," Mr Saunders apologised, glancing back at Kate. "It's a habit."

"Thomas," she replied, looking straight into his eyes. "It's Thomas but I would very much prefer Kate."

He gave her a reassuring smile and turned back to the young woman. "Kate is ready to complete the forms, but please speak to me before submitting them any further. We won't be following the usual procedures here." He turned to Kate and her children and shook each of their hands firmly. "It has been a pleasure to meet you all today. I look forward to you becoming part of our school family." He nodded and left Kate to complete the forms.

Twenty minutes later she was walking out of the school and down the steps with her children. It had been an emotionally exhausting morning, but it was done.

"Anyone for ice cream?" she said, giving her children a big hug.

"Yes," they said in unison, once again.

They sat at what had become their usual table in the diner. Jake and Lucy grabbed a window seat each and Kate slid in beside Lucy. Tina came across to take their order and there were the usual pleasantries while Jake and Lucy made what appeared to be a very difficult decision about which flavour of ice cream to have. Kate ordered coffee and a slice of the chocolate cake that had caught her eye when she walked in, a treat she felt she deserved today.

"Make that two please, Tina."

Startled, they all turned to see Matthew standing a few feet away. Tina gave an 'oh I can guess what's happened here' kind of smile as she finished writing on her pad before heading off to put their order together. Matthew stepped closer and looked at the empty seat next to Jake.

"May I join you?"

Jake looked at his mum. She nodded, and Jake budged up to let Matthew slide in beside him.

"What are you doing here, are you just passing or…?"

"I knew you were here."

"How?"

"Turns out my dad knows Walter," Matthew replied and left it at that.

Matthew had called Maggie a few times over the last two weeks to see how Kate was. Seeing her in the diner and wrapping his arms around her in the park had stirred up all his old feelings for her. However, this time they were only getting stronger and whether she was going to be part of his life or not he needed to make sure that she and her children were alright, one way or another.

Matthew turned to Jake and Lucy. "What have you been up to today?"

"We've been to see our new school," Lucy announced excitedly.

"Ah, and what did you all think of your new school?"

"It's small," replied Jake.

"It's all on one floor. There's no upstairs!" exclaimed Lucy.

Matthew laughed. "Yeah but it's a good school, it's where I went! I was in the soccer team. Do you play, Jake?"

Jake hung his head. "I don't," he muttered quietly. Matthew sensed not to take the subject any further and was saved by the arrival of ice cream and cake.

The four sat in the diner for almost two hours. It was all light-hearted, nothing deep. They chatted about what they liked about Colorado Springs and Jake and Lucy spoke enthusiastically about how the forests and the trees were so different to what they had been used to in New York.

"You will have to come and visit my ranch sometime if you like the forests and mountains."

"Yeah?" Lucy sat up excitedly.

"Yeah, we have the forest right behind us and then the mountains right behind the forest. There's cattle and horses and lots of space for running around."

Kate chipped in, "Well we start school tomorrow, so we are going to be busy."

It was all starting to feel a bit too comfortable for her. Everyone was chatting naturally and having a laugh. She knew she should be happy, but it felt strange. She could tell her children liked Matthew. They were both chatting freely, and Matthew had shown more interest in them in the last couple of hours than Adam had in years. She didn't understand why but she knew she didn't want them getting too close, too reliant on him being around when she had no idea what their future might hold.

She wondered if they felt safe. Kate always felt safe with Matthew, something she hadn't felt in years, but she knew she needed to stay focussed and independent. She still had to find a job and then somewhere to stay. They were still living in a guest house and that gave their lives a feeling of instability and uncertainty. That was a feeling she couldn't shake.

Matthew looked at his watch. "Oh, is that the time? I have to go."

"Aww," came two little voices.

"I have to help Dad this afternoon. The office has been neglected lately and we need to get the books up to date. I'm on computer duty – he hates that thing," he said, laughing.

"But I will maybe see you all again soon?" he added, glancing at Kate as he stood.

Kate smiled, not knowing what else to do. Her heart wanted her to stand up and throw her arms around him, have him wrap his strong comforting arms around her, but her head told her to stay seated. She knew he was interested in her and if she had a different past she might be able to let herself think about him that way too, but she and her children had been through enough.

She was brought from her thoughts by the lingering brushing of his lips against her forehead. She could feel her face flush red. Time seemed to stop. Her heart beat faster as she felt his warm breath on her skin. She could smell him. It was all so familiar. Her face flushed even redder when he pulled his lips away and she realised her eyes were still closed.

"Bye, Kate." Then, then there was that bloody smile.

Forty minutes later Matthew drew to a halt outside the ranch house. Running up the front steps he opened one of the wooden double doors and walked into the wide hallway. To the left was the spacious rectangular living room. Floor-to-ceiling windows, which framed the views to the front of the ranch house, bringing the natural beauty of outside in, were complemented by the solid wooden beams that crisscrossed the ceiling. An open fireplace stood in the middle of the facing wall with a Mexican-style rug in warm reds, ambers and oranges set out in front, luring you down to a selection of mix and match sofas and chairs. Some faced the fireplace while others made the most of the vast views. The wall to the right was shelved and adorned with row upon row of books which stopped only to make room for a piano which sat boldly between the books and the wall adjacent to the hallway. Trinkets that represented the four generations of the family were scattered about the room, giving it a stylish yet warm, homely feel.

Matthew tucked his head around the door directly opposite the living room. It was the office. His dad was sitting behind his desk working his way through what looked to be a never-ending mountain of paperwork.

"Well, did you see her?"

"Yeah." Matthew sighed as he walked across to his desk and sat down. Leaning forward he put his elbows on his desk and hung his head in his hands. "I love her, Dad. I love her, and I don't know if, after all she's been through, she will ever be able to let me back in. She relaxes, but then seems to remember and closes off again. I can't begin to imagine what her life has been like these past nine years, but I can tell it's been hell."

"What she needs now, son, is a friend. Someone she can trust who is on her side. Maybe after that things might move along."

"I know, and I will make sure she and her children are alright, even if she doesn't want me in her life."

"I know you will, son, I know you will."

After a moment's quiet reflection, John brought them from their thoughts. "Right, we had better get to work."

John was slowly coming to terms with the fact that everything had to be computerised but that certainly didn't mean he liked it. John had always run the business side of things himself and he was reluctant to hand that side over to Matthew. Not because he didn't trust Matthew to carry on the work he had done but because Wester Lakes was his life. He had poured his heart and soul into making it what it was today. When he had taken over from his father times had been hard and he had promised him that he would always fight to keep the business going.

Then when his wife died he had to fight to keep it going alone. In some ways that fight had played a big part in his healing process. It had kept him busy and over the years John had built the business up to be one of the most successful breeding and beef ranches in Colorado. The Harrison reputation spread far and wide and they were well respected in the community.

Now, though, John knew he had to move with the times. Most of their supplies were ordered and paid for online, companies were contacting them via email instead of letter and their banking was all done online too. Matthew had shown John how easy it would be if they had their budgets and projections on Excel spreadsheets rather than being handwritten as the math would be done for them, but John knew he would have to rely on Matthew until he got to grips with the computer. If he ever got to grips with it at all.

The two men worked together, Matthew creating files, scanning invoices and correspondence and John compartmentalising paperwork and tying this paper file with that paper file so that Matthew knew where the links were.

Matthew had already created the spreadsheets for the next five years' budgets and projections, so he set to work creating the online accounts sheets. Either he or his father would be able to go into them and update them daily, double-checking that their balance totals were in line with their budget sheets. They were all in one tab, allowing John to click back and forth from one page to another.

For the next two weeks the two men spent a few hours each afternoon in the office. Everything was finally online and they both agreed someone in the office a few hours a day would be handy. Their problem was that they wanted to oversee the financial side themselves, and they felt there wasn't quite enough work to hire someone for everything else. In the years before mobile phones they had needed someone there to take calls and John would go in at lunch and the end of the day to a pile of messages. Now, though, they answered calls and made decisions while they worked.

John and Matthew were managing the ranch together and that was working. They had a great respect for one another and had the same goals. They wanted the same things for the land and the animals, but they also knew they had scope to branch out and Matthew had an idea of how they could add a new dimension to their business to give them another source of income.

9

It was now the start of a new week and it had been a fortnight since Matthew had last seen Kate. Although desperate to see her he hadn't wanted to rush her, and he couldn't help but wonder if she had been thinking about him too. He was also keen to know how Jake and Lucy were settling into their new school. He had errands to run in town and thought it might be good to catch Kate on her own, while the children were in school. After a quick call to Maggie he jumped in his truck and headed into town.

Kate was sitting at what had become her usual table in the diner. She'd had a need for a familiar environment but being there without Jake and Lucy was not the same. She was missing them terribly when they were in school, but she knew she had to get used to it, become independent again.

She was so used to their little unit of three that she was now left feeling exposed, vulnerable and more alone than ever before. She knew she was down; she recognised the signs. She wasn't sleeping, she was becoming irritable and was feeling helpless. The strength she had managed to maintain all through her horrendous years in New York was now slipping. She was not depressed but she knew that was exactly where she was headed if she didn't get her life in order. A job and a permanent place to stay would make a huge difference, she was sure of that.

She had scoured the pages of yet another real estate guide and the job section of the local paper. There was nothing going work wise. Any management posts that aligned with her degree did not want a single mother who was fitting a job around her children. They wanted someone who was dedicated to the cause one hundred and ten percent, could work full days and travel here, there and everywhere at a moment's notice. The vacancies that did fit around school did not pay nearly enough. She couldn't pay rent, bills, food and clothing on the part-time hours that were currently available.

She was reluctant to register for benefits as her name and location would be out there in cyberspace for government departments to see. Could that help Adam find them if he wanted to? She had no idea.

She was still toying with the idea of setting up a small baking business from home, but she couldn't do that either until she had somewhere to stay and she couldn't afford somewhere to stay until she was working. Then there would be hygiene inspections and equipment, all of which would cost more money, money she didn't have. She was going around in circles. Every day was the same. Every day she knew what she needed to do but couldn't afford to do it.

Drastic action was needed. The money she had saved before leaving New York was now running desperately low. She was paying Maggie rent weekly and had the next two months set aside but she also knew she needed that money as a deposit when she found a place to live. The longer she stayed with Maggie and Walter the less deposit she would have. It was crunch time for her and her children and Kate knew it.

Hearing the diner door open she looked up. Matthew was walking towards her. She could tell he was happy to see her and the sight of him instantly cheered her up. He came towards her with a hand outstretched.

"Come with me," he said calmly, although his eyes were pleading with her, willing her to get up and follow him.

"Why, where are we going?"

"Come with me, please. I will have you back in time for school coming out, I promise."

Kate stood up, gathered her things, quickly paid for her coffee and followed him out of the diner. Not a word was said between them as they crossed the road and walked towards his truck. Matthew held Kate's door open and she jumped in. He then ran around the other side, got in and started the engine. Still not a word had been spoken as he drove off.

Kate looked out at the glorious views as they headed towards the mountains. The truck left the straight highway and turned onto a smaller country road. It twisted and turned as it followed the line of the mountains, climbing slowly through the trees and eventually coming out high above Colorado Springs. Still not a word had been spoken as Matthew turned off again, onto what was now nothing more than a track. He came to a halt at a viewpoint which looked back down the mountain.

Kate gasped at the view in front of her. Having dreamed of the mountains for so long, she now felt part of them. She gazed in wonder. Colorado Springs was far bigger than she had realised and for the first time she was getting a feel for where she was. She thought about her life there and how her children were there, right now at that very moment. Down there living a life so far away from what they had known before. Lifting her eyes, she looked out beyond Colorado Springs at the vast flat land spread out as far as her eyes could see. That was where she had come from. She had for the very first time a real sense of belonging. She felt she was having an out-of-body experience looking down at her new life from a great height. It didn't change the fact that there were no suitable jobs in her vicinity and she couldn't afford anything better than a hovel to live in, but she knew she wasn't going to give up.

Matthew had already jumped out of the truck and was heading round to open her door. She leaped out and he wrapped his jacket around her shoulders.

"It can get chilly up here," he said tenderly before taking her hand again and leading her towards an old wooden bench. Well worn and sheltered by tall spruce trees, its outlook was open. They sat down together both looking straight ahead. Matthew pointed to where the guest house, park, school and diner were, giving Kate an idea of her little patch of Colorado Springs.

"How have you been?" he asked.

"Fine." Kate's false reply didn't fool him.

"And Jake and Lucy, are they settling in at school?"

"Yes."

Silence. Matthew wondered if he would ever bring Kate back. Was she still angry at him because he had left New York and come home or was it because of the abuse she had suffered at the hands of Adam? Probably a bit of both, he thought. He was wondering what to say next, how to get her to relax and talk to him, when suddenly Kate broke the silence.

"Lucy more so than Jake but she's younger, less aware of what she's been through and what she's missed out on."

"Jake is still young, you will just have to give him time."

"I know. He never speaks about New York or his dad. Only once when we went to enrol at the school, that's the only time. I have no idea if he feels relaxed, happy and free or if more damage has been done than I've realised and he's keeping it all to himself."

"Has he joined any school clubs?"

"No. I think he would enjoy soccer, but he doesn't know the rules and I know that puts him off. Adam never played or watched it with him."

Matthew sat for a moment. "What about you? How are you feeling?"

Kate let out a sigh. "Life is so much better now. We are free. We can live. We can do and say whatever we want without having to worry about someone else's angry response."

"But...?" Matthew prompted.

"But, I can't find a job that works around school and still pays enough for us to get by. As for places to stay, well, all I can afford right now is a one-bedroom hovel."

Kate went on to tell Matthew about her thoughts on running a business from home.

"But who wants to buy cakes that are baked in a hovel?" She laughed. What else could she do?

Matthew fell silent. He hadn't realised her situation was quite so bleak financially. She could tell he was deep in thought but somehow his strong silence was reassuring. If she had dared to moan about any aspect of her life to Adam there would have certainly been a physical backlash.

Matthew took her hand again. "Come on, I want to show you something."

He led her a few metres along a stony path before turning into the forest. The sharp, sweet scent from the spruce trees reminded Kate of Christmas. The deep blue Colorado sky gave way to cool dark shade as she followed Matthew further into the forest. Lucky I've got flat shoes on, she thought to herself as she kept her gaze down, watching where she put her feet.

"It's not much further," Matthew reassured as he continued to lead the way.

"You're lucky I trust you," she joked, aware that the cool darkness now surrounded them.

A few minutes later the trees gave way again and eight feet of rugged rock jutted out in front of them. Matthew led Kate to a patch of rock that levelled out. She looked up, transfixed by the view that lay in front of her. The ledge they were standing on jutted out high above the trees they had driven through earlier. Kate felt as though she was being propelled out, out from the forest and into the wonders of the land below.

"It's beautiful. Absolutely beautiful," she said, turning to Matthew.

"It's my home."

"What?" she stuttered in disbelief. Not that she thought he was lying, Matthew wasn't like that, but because she was in awe at someone growing up in such a beautiful place.

He nodded. "Look down at the river snaking away from us. Now follow it into the distance."

Kate looked out and followed the river as it wound its way from them through the lush green fields and out into the drier plains. The sun's reflection was catching the water, making it sparkle as if to reinforce Matthew's instructions.

"Now keep following it way into the distance until you come to a hard right turn just before it disappears from sight."

"Okay, I see the right turn."

"Well from there, back up to the top of this tree line above us, and from the highway on the right all the way across to the top of the tree line on the left, is our land."

Kate looked out in wonderment. She knew the ranch would be big, but she had no idea that Matthew's family owned so much land.

"What an amazing place," she said, turning to face him. "I can see why you struggled to be away from here for too long and I get why you had to come back."

"My grandad used to bring me up here, onto this ledge. It was his favourite place in the whole world. My dad comes up here sometimes too, there's just something about it. I could sit up here for hours." Eventually he turned, and still holding Kate's hand, he led her back to the bench they had been sitting on earlier. This time, though, Kate was relaxed, and they sat facing each other.

"I want to run something by you, Kate. It's just an idea. No pressure and I promise I'm not making a move. I know you must make a life here properly for yourself and the kids but maybe I can offer you a solution."

Panic began to build inside her. She had no idea what he was about to say but she was enjoying having him in her life again and didn't want him to say something now that would spoil things.

"Please don't interrupt until I've got it all out. I want you to know absolutely everything before you react."

Kate looked at him, nodding reluctantly.

"You need a job and somewhere to live, somewhere that's not a hovel," he said jokingly. "Please, please don't jump to the wrong conclusion when I say this but there is plenty of room at the ranch." Matthew still had Kate's hand in his, he had never let it go, and he could feel it flinch slightly. "Dad and I have bedrooms upstairs, but there are bedrooms downstairs that would be perfect for you and the kids and there is a separate bathroom there too."

Kate stared at him. She was aware she was staring but she didn't know what else to do. She couldn't understand why her head wasn't spinning in panic as it always did. She couldn't understand why she wasn't slapping his suggestion down. She could only sit silently, watching as he offered her his world.

"You would all be welcome, Kate, you know that. Dad would enjoy having you and the kids around too, they would inject a bit of life into the place."

Kate was still looking at Matthew. That damn smile was there. It wasn't an arrogant smile, not an 'I'm the hero, here to solve all your problems' kind of smile. It was an 'I'm here for you' smile. He cared, not just about her but Jake and Lucy too, she knew that.

"Matthew, I can't. I can't afford to pay you a decent rent. I just can't. I would feel I was taking you for granted, using you, and you don't deserve that."

"Well…we could do with some help in the office. We've just moved everything onto the computer so it's easier, but we still need someone in there a few hours a day. Someone to keep it ticking over, secretarial but also helping a little with payroll, invoices, that kind of thing. And the vacancy just happens to come with accommodation for three," he added, smiling at her conspiratorially. "Look, Kate, it offers you an instant solution. A home, a job, and the kids would thrive out here. Emma would adore them."

"Emma?"

"Emma's our housekeeper. She sees to the housework,

cooks the meals, and I know she would love having another female around the house." Matthew went on to explain about Jesse, the other ranch hands and the occasional Sarah. "You don't have to answer now, take as long as you need," he said, stroking Kate's hand with his fingers. "But if it would help you could come over sometime, meet everyone, have a look around the house and the office, see what it entails, see if the kids like it too."

Kate took a deep breath. "Okay, but don't say a word to Jake or Lucy. Let them just think we're visiting you. I don't want them to know a thing until I've had time to think about this. Promise?"

"I promise. Look, Kate, I'm going to be honest with you. I love you. I always have. I know you know that, and I know deep down you love me too. I also know that nothing will happen between us unless you decide otherwise, that it might *never* happen. I'm offering you this as a friend. We go too far back, Kate, and I can help. No ties, no assumptions – you have your life, I have mine."

"Can we come this afternoon?"

"This afternoon?" Matthew spluttered. "Yes, yes, this afternoon's fine! Yes. We could go straight from school?" he suggested, tightening his hold on Kate's hand slightly. Kate could only nod.

Matthew was stunned at Kate's reaction; he had expected her to think about it and get back to him in a few days. Although she wasn't committing to anything other than a look around yet, of course.

Kate sat quietly looking out at the tranquillity before her. If she could have stopped time she would have. There were no problems up here on the mountain; she felt removed from them all. She had been as stunned as Matthew at her response, but everything felt right, and she knew she was almost out of options.

"Come on, I'd better get you back."

A short while later, Matthew sat in the truck while Kate waited at the school gate for Jake and Lucy. An afternoon of Matthew's company had been enough to lift her spirits and she was enjoying the warm Colorado sunshine. She watched as another mother arrived, a polite nod of acknowledgement and a smile, but Kate was struggling. Her years of isolation in New York had knocked her confidence hugely. Her fear of Adam had meant she'd spent those years trying to avoid contact with other parents. In the early years they would chat and invite her children for play dates, but she became known for always turning them down. After a while people stopped asking and eventually stopped talking to her altogether. The heartbreaking thing for Kate was that deep down she had craved their company. Here, however, she'd had a few hellos but nothing more and she knew she was going to have to do something about that.

10

Jake and Lucy were delighted to be going to the ranch. Lucy was excited at the prospect of seeing horses and Jake was full of questions about how the ranch was run. It was something completely different to anywhere they had ever been before and neither child knew just how much was riding on their visit.

Matthew turned the truck into the long driveway of Wester Lakes Ranch. Silence fell over the truck as Kate and her children looked out at the rolling fields and stunning mountain views. As Matthew continued up the driveway the children's eyes were drawn to the cattle in the distance and the horses grazing in the paddocks by the side of the driveway. Kate, however, was looking straight ahead at the ranch house nestled at the foot of the mountains.

"Matthew, it's beautiful. It's absolutely beautiful."

Matthew stayed quiet for a few minutes before carrying on past the ranch house. "I thought we might work backwards."

Kate and the children watched as the road curved round, passing the bunkhouses and outbuildings and away from the ranch house. The views were changing, though still just as stunning. Cody and Jason waved as the truck drove past. They were fixing a fence at the side of the road, which was now becoming a dirt track. Jake's and Lucy's eyes were like saucers.

"Look at the horses!" exclaimed Lucy. "And the tractor! What are they doing?"

Jake answered before Matthew had a chance. "I think they're taking food to the cattle."

"That's right, that will be Owen taking fresh feed over."

Kate knew her children were relaxed and happy. They were excited to be here, excited about what they could see, and they still hadn't stepped out of the truck. Matthew continued round towards the cattle sheds and stables and came to a halt.

"Okay, everybody out." He led Jake and Lucy across to a tall wooden fence that enclosed a small paddock beside one of the sheds.

"Wait here and I will bring someone to meet you."

Matthew disappeared into what Kate now realised was a stable. Minutes later he appeared out of a different door straight into the paddock. He was walking a small chestnut-brown pony with white knees and socks all ready to go with saddle and bridle. Eyes like saucers again, Lucy and Jake climbed up the fence for a closer look.

"Meet Annabel," Matthew said. "She hasn't had her fun today. Who would like to go first?"

"Me!" squealed Lucy, almost bursting with excitement.

"Come on then, climb over."

Lucy looked at her mum for permission, pleading to her with her eyes. Kate laughed and gestured to her to go. Matthew lifted Lucy onto Annabel's back.

"Comfy?"

Lucy nodded.

"We have to do this properly so that Annabel understands what we want her to do." Matthew shortened the stirrups so that Lucy's feet could reach into them and adjusted her so that she was in the right position. Then, taking the reins in his hands, "This is your steering wheel." He wrapped her little hands around the reins. "Keep your hands like this, okay?"

Lucy nodded vigorously; it was all she could do. Excitement had taken over.

"Ready?"

Again, Lucy could only nod. Twenty minutes later Lucy had walked, trotted and had a small canter round the paddock. Kate watched as her daughter's initial apprehension gave way to utter joy. Matthew had control of Annabel the whole time, but Lucy had done as Matthew had asked, each time giving little commands with her feet and the reins when told. Kate could feel herself becoming emotional and watched as Matthew helped Lucy down from Annabel and adjusted the stirrups again for Jake.

"Come on then, your turn," Matthew called to Jake.

"Now I think you're tall enough to mount Annabel yourself, let's see." He signalled Jake over to Annabel's side and had a quick measure with his eyes. "Okay, Jake, put your hands here and here." He signalled to the front and back of the saddle. "And your left foot in here," he instructed, holding the stirrup out steady. "Now hold on tight to the saddle, it won't move, and push your foot down into the stirrup as hard as you can and try to pull yourself up."

Jake held on tight. His fingers dug into the tough leather as he pushed his foot as hard as he could down into the stirrup. He felt his other foot leave the ground.

"That's it, keep going." Matthew knew when Jake would struggle and just before Jake felt he couldn't lift himself up any more Matthew grabbed his thigh and gave him a push upwards. Just enough to propel Jake up so he could put his other leg across the pony's back and down the other side.

"Brilliant. And look at those feet – you have been listening." Matthew helped him with the reins and then led him forward.

Kate and Lucy watched as Matthew progressed Jake from a walk to a trot, then to a canter. Kate could tell Jake was enjoying it far more than she had thought he would and found herself becoming emotional, once again, at the obvious joy on his face. She thought about how much her children had missed out on in their short lives and how wonderful it was to see someone other than herself, Maggie or Walter showing her children kindness.

"Hello, Kate."

Dragged from her thoughts Kate turned to see John walking out from the stable towards her. He looked older, his dark hair now rather more salt than pepper, but he was still a fit and handsome man for his age.

She rushed towards him and gave him a hug. "Hello, John, it's so nice to see you."

"You too, it's been far too long, Kate, far too long," he replied, still holding her by the arms. "And my goodness, who do we have here?"

"This is Lucy," Kate replied, turning and waving to Lucy to come over.

"Hello, Lucy, how was Annabel, did you have fun?"

"She was great," Lucy replied before giving John a minute-by-minute account of her entire experience.

Laughing they turned and walked back towards the fence to watch Jake. He was just finishing a small canter and Matthew was full of praise for him.

"Quite a natural there," John said, nudging Kate's elbow. "You would think he'd done that before."

Kate smiled. She knew that trying something different would be good for both her children, but especially Jake. She needed to encourage him to be a little braver.

"You will all be coming back to the house for dinner later?" John continued.

Kate looked at him, not knowing how to answer. It struck her right there and then that she was always unnerved by people's kindness. She had spent so long with Adam, who always had an ulterior motive for everything, that now when people were genuinely showing her kindness, she found herself doubting them, looking for that ulterior motive. Deep down though she knew John had no motive; he was one of the nicest people she had ever met. A good head for business, took no nonsense, but at the same time a warm family man. John had visited Matthew regularly while he was at university in New York and Kate had met him often over the three years she and Matthew had dated. She had often thought of him too over the years, hoping life was being kind to him.

Kate glanced across at Matthew. She had no idea how he would feel about them staying for dinner.

"Oh, I don't—"

John interrupted before she could finish. "Come on, it's been years and you're here anyway. You would make Emma's day – she loves to feed people." He began walking back towards the stable. "I'll see you at the house later," he shouted over his shoulder.

"Mum, mum!" Jake came running over. "That was amazing! Can we come back and do it again, please?"

Kate laughed as she hugged him. "We shall see."

"Jake, Lucy, would you like to help me put Annabel back in her stable?" Matthew asked.

Jake and Lucy climbed the fence, this time without the backwards glance for their mother's approval. Kate watched as the three of them disappeared out of sight. They had only been at the ranch an hour, but she and her children felt relaxed and free. Leaning on the fence she looked across the green fields and back towards the ranch house. Her eyes were drawn up beyond the trees to the mountains behind. She could almost pick out the spot where she and Matthew had sat earlier that day looking down at where she was now. She could not have felt further away from New York at that moment and she could almost feel the ranch breathing new life into her.

The sound of laughter brought her from her thoughts; she couldn't see into the stable, but she could hear the lively chatter. Matthew had been wonderful with Jake and Lucy, especially Jake. He had quietly encouraged, with no fuss, and that was exactly what Jake needed.

She looked back at the house, and Kate knew she had a decision to make. Not the obvious one about whether to accept Matthew's offer or not – that decision was a no-brainer. Deep down she knew she would have no choice but to accept. There was a job that she knew she could do. Her business degree would be ideal, and admin was admin to her. She would just have to learn the ranch side of the office. There was a home, an amazing home, and her children would flourish here, of that she was sure. Plus there would be an instant family of sorts.

Her problem was Matthew. He did not deserve to be led on, to give his life up in the hope of her. She also wanted to be happy, and if she was being honest there was no one else she would rather be with, but giving in to him, giving herself over to him, was not something she could contemplate yet. Adam had left Kate so battered and bruised physically and emotionally that she had to find herself first. Become stronger in herself before she could give herself to someone else. Even if that someone was Matthew.

Kate turned quickly to the sound of more laughter. Matthew and her children were walking out from the main door of the stable towards her.

"I believe you're staying for dinner."

"Is that okay? Your dad was pretty insistent."

"Of course. Come on then, let's finish the tour." He nodded towards the truck. Jake and Lucy ran ahead eagerly and jumped in as Matthew and Kate walked slowly behind.

"They had a great time with Annabel and I know what you did with Jake, thank you."

Matthew smiled and opened Kate's door for her. She jumped in and watched as he walked round the front of the truck. His dark, slightly wavy hair was always short and neat. His rugged handsome features encased deep blue eyes that laughed when he did. Then there was the smile, that irresistible smile. She couldn't help but wonder why no one else had snapped him up in the years since his divorce.

They continued their tour of the ranch, taking in the cattle sheds, pastures, drier plains and the river that snaked its way through the land. Matthew explained to Jake how they used the river for irrigation, how it was so integrally important to the survival of their ranch and to the cattle and horses. Then he turned and drove back past the old unused bunkhouses, cattle sheds and stables towards the main outbuildings and ranch house.

Instead of parking Matthew turned onto a dirt track and Jake and Lucy watched excitedly as he drove up into the forest that was nestled behind the ranch buildings at the foot of the mountain. He drove upwards on a track that wound its way back and forth though the trees. Matthew explained that they farmed the trees in an ongoing cycle of cutting down and replanting. That they varied in age and would be cut down in stages and the wood sold.

Turning again he drove them back down the bumpy track and pulled to a stop in front of the ranch house. Jumping out of the truck, Matthew walked them round the outbuildings, explaining what each was for. He pointed out a few no-go areas to the children where they kept veterinary supplies, feeds, fertilisers and machinery before walking them back towards the ranch house.

A couple of trucks and a tractor were heading their way.

"Ah, it must be time for dinner," Matthew said, rubbing his hands together. "You hungry?" he asked, looking at Jake and Lucy.

"Yes!"

"Come on then, follow me." Matthew turned to look at Kate. He could tell she was nervous. He put his hand gently on her back and whispered, "It's going to be fine, I promise."

The four of them headed up the steps towards the front door. "We usually go in the back way when we've been out on the ranch, but the lads will all be piling in the back doors and getting cleaned up for dinner, so we'll go in this way." Matthew took his mucky boots off, and Kate, Jake and Lucy did the same, setting their shoes and sneakers beside his boots before following him inside.

Jake and Lucy gasped as they walked into the hallway,

which was bigger than their room at the guesthouse. Their eyes swivelled as they were drawn to the hand-crafted wooden staircase and the solid wooden beams that criss-crossed the ceiling.

"Follow me," Matthew said, leading the way. "Dad has told Emma you're coming so there will be places set for you at the table."

He led them through a door at the opposite end of the hallway which opened into a large open-plan area. Kitchen to the right and dining area with boot room and toilet for the ranch hands to the left. Kate looked around at the vast open space that wouldn't look out of place in a country living brochure.

The kitchen had wooden cupboards which complemented the solid beams running across the ceiling. Light from the windows which looked out to the mountains behind was reflected on the pale granite worktops. An island sat as if closing off the kitchen from the dining area and was currently set up with dishes for dinner while the dining area was dominated by a rectangular solid wood table. French doors on the left led outside to the wooden veranda that circled the house. Kate could see the row of men's mucky boots which had been abandoned outside as Matthew ushered her and her children to wash their hands before returning to the table.

Some of the seats were taken. Cody and Blake were just finishing washing their hands and Emma was rushing about in a calm, organised manner.

"Come in, come in," John said, rising from his seat. "We

have guests this evening. This is Kate and her children, Jake and Lucy. Kate's an old friend of the family – she and Matthew knew each other years ago back in New York."

He went on to introduce everyone in turn, explaining a little about what they did before introducing Emma. "And this is Emma. I have no idea what we would do without her." He smiled at her as she placed the last of the dishes in the centre of the table.

"Welcome, welcome," she said, wiping her hands on her apron while bustling round the table towards Kate. "The more the merrier."

Kate scanned the table. John was seated furthest away at the head of the table and the chairs were filled either side of him by Blake, Cody, Owen, Jason, Dylan and Jesse. Matthew gently took Kate's elbow and led her towards the empty end of the table. There were two chairs that backed onto the kitchen with another two directly opposite. Kate looked on nervously, wondering where to sit when Lucy climbed onto a chair facing the kitchen – it had armrests and Kate knew that was the clincher for her. Kate took the empty chair beside her while Jake and Matthew sat opposite.

"I hope you're hungry – there's plenty to choose from. We have a speciality tonight," Emma announced, winking at Lucy. "We have roast beef, but we also have mac 'n' cheese and there are potatoes and some mixed vegetables. Just tuck in," she instructed, taking the seat beside Jesse.

Kate watched her children. They were used to sitting at a little table, four of them until recently, then three. Now they were part of what she could only imagine looked like a banquet to them. The ranch hands were obviously hungry, and she could tell Emma had a full-time job keeping them all fed. But the atmosphere was casual and relaxed, and Kate very quickly felt at ease.

She helped Lucy put some mac 'n' cheese on her plate, and she picked out a potato, some carrots and a piece of broccoli for her. Lucy's face fell at the addition of the vegetables, but she knew better than to complain so she mixed them in with her mac 'n' cheese, hoping to drown out any hint of their existence. Kate looked across at Jake, who was helping himself to the potatoes; Matthew had put a slice of roast beef on his plate when he was getting his own. He had avoided the vegetables altogether and Kate reached over and put some at the side of his beef. Jake glanced up at his mum and laughed; he should have known he would never have gotten away with it.

Dishes were passed back and forth across the table until everyone had full plates. The conversation was light and friendly, and everyone was included. They asked Jake and Lucy about their school and teachers. The young ranch hands had plenty to say on the subject as they had all been through the same school themselves. Some of their teachers were still there and they were full of stories about things they had gotten up to. Some good, some not so good, but all resulting in Kate and her children laughing and relaxing into the group.

Once plates were emptied, the ranch hands sat back relaxed while Emma cleared the table. Kate felt awkward.

"Let me help," she said, getting to her feet. She gathered

up the plates and cutlery from her end of the table and followed Emma over to the kitchen.

"Take these, dear," Emma said, giving Kate pudding plates.

There's more? Kate thought to herself. She was full after her main course.

Emma took a large chocolate cake from the counter and headed towards the table. "Bring the plates here, please. I'd better cut this myself or there will be nothing left for the rest of us." She gave the ranch hands a cheeky wink and chuckled as she placed the cake in her own spot at the table. "I'll cut if you pass the plates around, dear," Emma instructed as she sliced into the cake. It was deep and moist, layered with chocolate cream and topped with chocolate shavings. Jake and Lucy could barely take their eyes off it as Emma sliced and plated until everyone had a piece. Silence fell across the table as everyone indulged in what could only be described as chocolate heaven.

"This is delicious, Emma," Kate complimented quietly.

Emma gave her a gentle smile. As soon as everyone was finished the ranch hands thanked Emma and headed back out to work.

"See you all at supper," she shouted after them.

Startled, Kate looked across at Matthew. "Supper?"

"Yes, they get all their meals here. When they start working for us, they get the choice between having full pay or a slight reduction in pay and all meals provided. If anyone does choose full pay it's never for very long," he laughed. "This way we know everyone is well fed, especially the younger ones, and we all eat at the same time which works better for the running of the ranch. It lets us all catch up, get to know each other and if anything needs talking over or sorted out from during the day we can do it then."

Kate stood up to help Emma clear the table as John popped his head back in the veranda door.

"I'm heading over to check the cattle, alright if I take Jake and Lucy along?"

They looked at their mother, pleading with their eyes for the second time that day. "Okay but be careful. Remember your sneakers are at the front door."

Lucy ran over and gave her mum a hug before following her brother out into the hallway.

"Off you two go too, I can take care of all this," Emma instructed in a matter-of-fact tone. Kate wasn't completely at ease with Emma. She didn't know why as Emma had been nothing but friendly and welcoming towards them and the mac 'n' cheese had obviously been made for her children's benefit. But Kate still felt that she and her children were intruding a little.

"Please let me help, there are so many dishes."

"Don't worry, dear, Mr Harrison has blessed me with two dishwashers. They will be done in no time, honestly, off you go."

Matthew laughed. "You won't win. Come on, I'll show you around the rest of the house."

11

Kate followed as Matthew led her into the living room.

"It's all so big," she said, taking in the welcoming fireplace, the rows of books and the piano. "Do you play?"

"A little. I'm rusty but I get by."

Kate wandered towards the window nearest the fireplace and looked out over the ranch. Matthew followed and pointed to his dad's truck in the distance. The dry dust was being churned up behind and she knew her children would be having a great time with John.

As Matthew stood beside her he could feel her presence in a way he hadn't felt in years. There was always an underlying sexual tension between them. They both felt it and knew the other felt it too, but they both stood quietly looking out at the endless views, content to be in each other's company.

Eventually Matthew took her hand. "Come on, I'll show you the rest."

He led Kate back into the hallway and straight across to the office. The large room was fitted out with two desks, two filing cabinets, a tall three-door cupboard and a long bench with a printer, laminator and two three-tier racks full of paperwork. It was tidy enough though didn't appear to be overly organised.

"If you want to run now I'll understand," he joked, taking her further into the room. "I know you still have to decide but let me show you around in here, give you a feel for it, see if you think you would like it or not. That's Dad's desk over there." Matthew pointed to the older, more cluttered desk on the opposite wall. It looked as though it was as old as the house and Kate presumed it had belonged to earlier generations who had run the ranch. "And this is my desk." Matthew walked across to the larger desk by the side of the window. It faced into the room but was angled so that the sunlight didn't reflect on the computer screen and that Matthew could still see out. It looked out towards the outbuildings and Kate could see Jason and Dylan going in and out as they got on with their work. There was a bustling feel to it, in the house but still part of the business outside.

"As I mentioned earlier, everything – accounts, budgets, banking – has just gone onto the computer so that is all new to Dad. The racks on the bench there, one has invoices. We usually put them there until we have time to check that we've received everything we've been invoiced for before paying it. The other rack is for incoming mail and things that need to be dealt with. We sort of use it – I feel it's easier to put things on our desks where we can see them rather than over there, but we can think about that. I'd hand my desk over to you if you took on the job and I'd use the bench, put a chair there and move the racks."

Matthew sat down and leaning back in his chair put his hands behind his head. "Dad has run the office since Mum died and has had to fit it in around everything else. As the ranch has expanded so has the office workload and he just doesn't have the time. He knows he needs to hand some things over but it's hard for him and I'm trying to share the load with him but in a way that doesn't make him feel like I'm taking over or that he's losing his grip. It's just become far too much now and I'm not the most efficient person to have in an office either," he said, laughing. "Although the computer side of things, I'm a whiz." He grinned and gave Kate a wink.

Kate walked across and leaned against the edge of the desk beside him. "You're a good man, Mr Harrison, with a kind heart." His deep blue eyes smiled back at her. "Admin is admin. It won't take long to get things sorted out in here."

Matthew tried to work out if that was an acceptance of his offer or simply a general comment. He watched as she scanned the room, her mind ticking over. He knew that the old Kate would be working out what should be done first, making lists and placing tasks in order of importance. He hoped the new Kate was doing the same.

"Enough of in here, let me show you the rest," and taking Kate by the hand again, Matthew led her out of the office.

Directly to the right was another hallway. Kate wondered how she hadn't noticed it earlier when she'd come in but guessed she'd been too busy admiring the wooden beams on the ceiling.

"There are three bedrooms down here, each with a small shower room and a bathroom."

He led Kate into the first bedroom which backed onto the office. It was a good size, square, and had a window looking out over the front of the ranch. There were two doors on the far wall; one was the shower room and the other a spacious closet with shelves and hanging space. A double bed, two chests of drawers and a night stand barely filled the room. She followed Matthew to the bedroom next door. It was identical to the previous bedroom but with the shower room and closet on the nearest wall.

"These two would be perfect for Jake and Lucy as the next room is bigger."

Matthew led Kate across the hallway to the last bedroom. It was about half the size again and as well as a double bed and bedroom furniture it had a small sofa sitting at a door which led out to the back of the house. It opened onto the veranda with views to the mountains. There were two chairs and a small round table sitting just outside the door and across to the left was the entrance to the dining area of the kitchen. There was an overhang that surrounded the house and covered the veranda. Kate could feel herself welling up as Matthew showed her the double closet and shower room. It was beautiful, and she couldn't think of a more perfect place to live.

"Come on, I'll show you the bathroom." He led her next door. The white bathroom suite was complemented by light marble tiles and a two-door shelved closet.

"Obviously if you decided to come here we would get towels and bedding in here. No one uses these rooms anymore, so they just sit here."

"That's such a shame, they're so beautiful."

"I know. Years ago when the house was fuller they were all used, but my grandparents died, and then because I was so young when my mum died I've no brothers or sisters. It's just Dad and me." He shrugged his shoulders. "It is what it is, but Dad and I have done alright. Let me show you upstairs. Then we might have time for a walk before the kids get back."

Kate followed Matthew back out into the main hallway. She walked with him up the beautifully carved wooden staircase. She was enjoying spending time with him, having him completely to herself again, even if it was just for a little while.

He pointed to a door which Kate decided was directly above the living room: "That's Dad's bedroom," before leading her into a room directly behind at the rear of the house, "And this is his den. He loves this room."

The wooden beams arced beautifully, coming to a point in the centre of the ceiling. Windows swallowed the mountain views from behind and an open fireplace sat on the same wall as the door they had just entered. Two sofas and a coffee table sat invitingly in front of the fireplace. Bookshelves lined every inch of the walls, breaking only for doors and windows. Kate looked around the room, struggling to take it all in. It was breathtaking.

Matthew took her hand again and led her back out into the hallway and across the landing. He pointed to another door directly opposite the top of the staircase. "That's another bathroom." Then he led her to the final door.

She had expected another hallway, as if to mirror downstairs, but instead there was a solid wall and a single door.

"This is my room." The usual confident Matthew had gone, and a vulnerable, uncertain expression had spread across his face. "I don't know whether to show you or not. I don't want you to get the wrong idea."

"Oh, for goodness' sake," she laughed, "you've shown me everything else, why stop now?"

Matthew opened the door and led her inside. Kate stood, her mouth open. "Bloody hell, Matthew," she exhaled. "This isn't a bedroom, it's a suite."

"It was my grandparents', their space when they were alive."

She looked around, trying to take in what lay before her. There were two sofas in front of her, one facing a fireplace that was on the same wall as the door she had just entered and the other, still taking in the fireplace, but facing the first of three floor-to-ceiling windows, making the most of the views out to the front of the ranch. To the rear of the room were double doors leading out to a balcony which sat above the dining area downstairs and looked towards the mountains. There was a desk and bookshelves on the far wall and another door. Matthew led Kate towards the other door and through to his bedroom. To her left was a bathroom followed by a row of closets lining the back wall. His bed was centred on the facing wall and floor-to-ceiling windows again swallowed the views to the front of the ranch. Kate stood speechless; standing in his bedroom brought home to her his personal side. He wasn't just Matthew Harrison from Wester Lakes Ranch. It made her realise what he might be giving up if she and her children were to move in: his chance at happiness, of meeting someone, of marriage and children of his own.

Matthew worried he had overwhelmed her, but she needed to know what she was coming to if she took him up on his offer. Matthew's approach had always been to be open and honest. It was a quality Kate had always admired but now, this time around, she found it reassuringly refreshing. It was in stark contrast to her existence in New York.

Kate was drawn to the windows and their intoxicating view. The light was starting to fade but the views were still vast and calming.

Matthew's pocket beeped; he pulled out his mobile phone to find a text from his dad.

"Dad's asking if it's okay if they check the horses before they head back?"

Kate nodded and Matthew quickly replied.

"We have about thirty minutes before they're back. We could go for a walk or sit outside?"

"A walk would be nice." Kate smiled. "But we have to talk."

"Okay," Matthew replied hesitantly. They walked back towards the staircase in silence. They left the ranch house and Matthew led Kate back down the driveway and onto a path that followed the start of the tree line away from the house.

"There are no ears here," he joked nervously.

"It's beautiful here, Matthew, you are so lucky to have grown up here, to be part of all this."

"But?"

She stopped, turned to face him and took his hands in hers. "We both know we love each other. We both know we always have but I'm in no fit state for a relationship. I can't come here, work here, live here and bring my children here, because what happens if you find someone else in the meantime? You more than deserve that chance but what would happen to all of us then?"

"I can stop you right there." His tone had changed; it was raised, almost scared and his expression one of raw emotion. "You have no idea the effect you've had on my life, Kate. No idea what it was like coming back here without you all those years ago. Yes, I married, but my heart was never in it. She was nice, she was kind, but she wasn't you. She wasn't you, Kate. Look around you. Having all this brings women out of the woodwork, believe you me, and they have thrown themselves at me in the four years I've been back. But I haven't dated any of them, Kate. None, because none of them were you. So, if you are in no place for a relationship that's fine. I will respect that for as long as I live but I will be going nowhere else. My heart is here for you and you alone. If you don't want me I will have to live with that, but I will do it alone and single." Tears welled in his eyes. "If one day you decide you feel differently, that you want me, then you let me know. I can't be with another woman when I love you, Kate. I just can't. I tried that once and it didn't work."

Tears were now running down both their faces.

"How can I move here now?" she sobbed. "How can I possibly move here when you feel that way and be around you every day? I would feel I was slowly torturing you."

"Because you feel the same way too, Kate. You feel the same way, only Adam has hurt you so badly you aren't ready to move on. But are you not better here amongst friends, amongst people who care about you and Jake and Lucy, than out in some hovel on your own barely able to make ends meet?"

Kate looked at Matthew, at his tears. How did her life get to this point? To the point where she was hurting the only man she had ever truly loved. Her frustrations weren't with him, they were with Adam and herself. She knew that she was the only person standing in the way of her own happiness.

"Oh, Kate." He pulled her close and wrapped his arms around her and for the first time she wrapped her arms around him.

"I'm so sorry, I'm so sorry," she repeated.

"Don't be sorry. Scream and shout at me all you want if it helps but please come here, please. Let me take care of you. Let me love you like you deserve to be loved."

Kate pulled back to look at him, at the sincerity in his eyes. Deserve to be loved. She didn't feel she deserved anything, ever. Her expectations from life and people had become so low that someone saying those words, to *her*, was like a bolt of lightning striking her in the back and jolting her back into reality.

For once, Matthew couldn't read her expression. Kate lowered her head, tears still streaming down her face, and her voice trembled.

"My feelings for Adam went years ago but, but he—" She broke off to sob uncontrollably into his shoulder.

"He what, Kate, he what?"

Her knees gave way and she fell to the ground shaking. He fell with her. She couldn't look at him. She couldn't look into those deep blue eyes.

"He what, Kate?"

"He would take me regularly as if asserting his ownership and I let him. It was the safest way. If I stayed quiet, if I let him do it and didn't scream, the children wouldn't hear."

Matthew held her tight and rocked her back and forth. He couldn't comprehend how anyone could do what Adam had done. He felt rage. He felt pain. He felt an unconditional love for the woman in his arms. But he now understood their relationship. Their love, their connection, their inexplicable understanding of each other and why Kate hadn't allowed them to take their connection further.

"I'm here, Kate, I will always be here. I love you," he sobbed, tightening his hold.

Her sobs were too loud for her to hear his words, but his arms wrapped around her made her feel safe, safer than she had ever felt. She fell deeper into him and they held each other. Both silent, both hurting.

12

It was early the following Saturday that Walter and Maggie were helping Kate and her children bring the last of their belongings out to Matthew's truck. Matthew watched as Kate and her children said emotional goodbyes to the couple who had, in only a few short months, become like family. The bond between Kate, Maggie and Walter was deep and Kate knew that her young family had breathed new life into the elderly couple. It was a relationship that would continue, Kate was adamant about that.

Matthew shook Walter's hand and gave Maggie a hug before checking Jake and Lucy were settled into their seats in the back of his truck. Maggie gave Kate a wink. Kate knew Maggie more than approved of her move and Kate was surprised at how much that mattered to her. Everyone waved politely as Matthew drove off, but Kate knew everyone's emotions were running high.

The Colorado sunshine was warm and bright as Matthew turned the truck into the long driveway of Wester Lakes. The chatter from the back seat was full of excitement as Jake and Lucy again looked out at the grazing cattle and horses. Matthew stretched across and, as if to reassure her, took Kate's hand in his. She was looking straight ahead but gently placed her other hand on top of his and clasped his hand in hers. It was a small show of affection, but Matthew knew it was a giant leap of faith for Kate.

As Matthew pulled up outside the ranch house he spotted John sitting on the veranda. "This is an early break for you, Dad."

"I wanted to be here to welcome you all and help with the bags."

John joined Matthew as he opened the rear door of the truck. John's attempts at hiding his shock failed as he looked firstly at the trunk's lack of contents and then at Matthew. "Is this it?" he mouthed.

Matthew nodded and John turned his attention to Kate as she helped her children out of the truck.

"Welcome, my dear."

"Hello, John, I can't thank you enough for letting us stay here. I, I really can't."

"Oh nonsense, I should be thanking you. I'm hoping this means I never have to turn on that blasted computer again," he chuckled.

Matthew grabbed their bags from the truck and only slightly laden led them inside. "Right. Do we know whose bedroom is whose?"

"Mum said mine was the first one and Lucy's was at the end," Jake piped up.

"Okay, this is your room then, Jake." Matthew pushed the door open with his foot and let Jake walk in first.

Jake's eyes scanned the room. He couldn't have hidden his delight even if he had wanted to. Kate looked around: a desk, bookcase and small television had been added since she had first seen the room. All still matching, like it had always been there.

"I will leave you to explore…" Matthew said, putting Jake's rucksack and small bag down against his bed. "Come on, Lucy, let's find your room."

Lucy skipped down the hallway behind Matthew.

"Here we are." Again, Matthew pushed the door open and let Lucy walk in first.

"It's the same as Jake's!" she announced in delight. She'd had the smallest room in New York as she was the youngest, so this was quite a surprise. "And I can see the fields!" she added, running across to the window before turning and running back to Matthew. She barely came up to the middle of his thighs, but she threw her arms around them and hugged them tightly. She was still young enough to have no real idea of what had happened in the last few months or the preceding years. Her youthful innocence had been her protector.

Matthew set her rucksack and bag down. "I'll leave you to explore while I show your mum her room."

Lucy nodded excitedly and headed towards her closet to investigate.

Matthew opened the door directly opposite and stood back to let Kate walk in. She tried desperately to fight back tears as she looked around the room. It was beautiful. Some trinkets had been added since she had last seen it, and a desk and television. A small table had been put beside the sofa and some artwork had been hung on the walls.

"Emma has filled one of the closets in the bathroom with towels and bedding. If all your towels and laundry go into the baskets in the bathroom Emma will collect it daily, that way she won't disturb you. She's happy to see to it, she'll just add it in with ours."

"Oh goodness," Kate gasped, bringing her hands to her face as if to hide her humiliation. "I have to talk to Emma. I don't expect her to do our laundry. God only knows what that woman thinks of me."

Matthew laughed. "Emma is efficient and whizzes about the place at full speed and her facial expression is often stern, like a woman on a mission. But she's a big softy, you'll see. She is so busy trying to mother and take care of everyone that she forgets to stop and breathe sometimes."

Matthew set Kate's bag down and walked towards her. He wrapped his strong arms around her and for the second time she wrapped her arms around him too and rested her head on his shoulder. She could feel the warmth of his body on hers and a reassuring calmness spread across her. They stood for a few minutes before Matthew broke the silence. "Emma always has lunch ready at twelve-thirty. I'll leave you and the kids to unpack and I'll be in the kitchen if you need me," he said, leaning in and kissing her tenderly on the forehead before heading out the door.

Kate looked across at her bag of belongings. It would take her no time at all to unpack and would scarcely fill a chest of drawers, never mind the dream double closet that stood empty as if to reaffirm her situation. Deciding to leave that depressing task for later she walked out into the hallway and popped her head round Lucy's door. Empty. That's strange, she thought to herself, as she walked down the hallway and popped her head round Jake's door.

"Hey, Mum, have you seen this?" Jake gushed, opening the door to his own shower room.

"I have one too!" Lucy exclaimed, holding onto Jake's T-shirt with one hand and a teddy with the other.

"Where did you get the teddy?" Kate asked.

"It was in my closet."

"I have Lego in my closet!" Jake opened the other door to reveal a large box of Lego and an assortment of board games that looked as though they had been in the family for years.

Kate helped them unpack their clothes, a task which didn't take long at all, before showing them the bathroom and where the clean towels were kept. "We have about thirty minutes until lunch. Would you like to go for a walk, maybe see the horses?"

"Yes!"

Kate laughed as she ushered them towards the front door, their two little voices always in unison.

"Can Matthew come?" Lucy asked, looking at her mum with the same pleading look in her eyes that she'd had when she rode Annabel.

"Well, he can if he's not busy, but I think it would be nice for the three of us to have a little walk together just to see how we're all feeling. It's been an eventful morning."

Jake and Lucy followed their mum as she led them across the road towards a wooden fence that edged a large paddock. Her children were full of excitement as they looked across at the cattle grazing in the distance and the horses chilling in the midday sun. Slowly they wandered down the edge of the paddock towards the outbuildings as they chatted about their bedrooms and the ranch. Jake had obviously been paying attention when he was out checking the cattle with John as he was giving Kate all sorts of snippets of information. Her children were looking happy and relaxed. Happy and relaxed was all Kate had ever wanted for them.

Blake and Owen waved as they drove past, and Cody stopped to say hello and chat to Jake and Lucy as he walked back towards the ranch house from one of the outbuildings.

"Oh, that must be everyone coming back for lunch." Kate quickly ushered her children back to the house and straight into their bathroom to wash their hands. As she held the towel out for her children to dry their hands she could feel a nervous ache grip her stomach, as though someone had reached in and grabbed it and was now squeezing it as tightly as they could. A wave of nausea spread across her. She knew that Matthew would never tell anyone about her past but at the same time she knew they would all be wondering, maybe coming to their own conclusions, and goodness only knows what those conclusions might be.

She was not a gold-digger, not one for glamour or possessions, but they didn't know that. They knew nothing about her, only that she and Matthew knew each other years ago and now she was here, with two young children and not a lot else. Taking a deep breath, she walked her children towards the kitchen.

13

It was now their first Monday at Wester Lakes and Kate's alarm had sprung to life. Jumping out of bed she quickly ran into the shower – they all had a big day ahead of them. Matthew had taken himself out of the ranch rota and was going to run Kate and the children to school before spending the rest of the day in the office with Kate.

She emerged from the shower moments later and brushed her hair. She was able to blow-dry it today without worrying about waking her children. What a luxury, she thought to herself as she transformed her wet locks into her preferred effortless elegant style.

Half an hour later she was dressed, had applied a little make-up and was crossing the hallway to Lucy's bedroom. Kate looked at her daughter, tiny in her double bed. She was sound asleep and still clutching the teddy she had found in her closet. Gently Kate shook her shoulder.

"Lucy, Lucy. Time to get up for school."

Slowly her daughter opened her eyes.

"Come on, you have to get up, I have to go and wake your brother."

Kate walked down the hallway towards Jake's room. Light was streaming from under his doorway and Kate opened his door to find his curtains open, and Jake standing at his window watching the men outside.

"Hey, Mum. John's already been down to the stables and Cody is fixing that bit of veranda beside the door."

"Good grief. How long have you been up?"

"Not that long."

"Well it's time to get ready for school," she instructed, giving him a hug. "Go and get washed and clean your teeth. Your clothes are laid out on your chair. I'll go and make sure your sister's up – keep your fingers crossed!" she joked.

Half an hour later her two children were standing in front of her, school bags in hand and wearing two happy smiles. She laughed as she pulled them both in towards her for one giant hug. "Come on, let's go get breakfast."

Matthew was waiting for them in the kitchen. He was standing with his back to them, mug of coffee in hand, looking out the window. Kate stopped and watched him for a moment. She looked at his broad shoulders. They gave way to strong arms and his tall stature and good looks meant he had a presence. People noticed him wherever he went. To Kate though, it was also about who he was on the inside.

Suddenly aware of them standing there he turned to greet them. She was slightly embarrassed; she had no idea if she had been caught looking but she was saved from her blushes as the veranda doors swung open and John came in followed by the ranch hands. The room suddenly filled with chatter and everyone was rushing around, washing their hands and piling round the table. A blonde girl, who Kate presumed was the occasional Sarah, rushed in, said her good mornings, gave Kate and her children a pleasant smile and a wave as if introducing herself in a hurry before grabbing a couple of pancakes and rushing out again. Kate looked around nervously as she carefully ushered her children to their seats. She still had to get to grips with the routine of the house.

John watched from the far end of the table as Matthew poured another mug of coffee and took it over to Kate.

"Morning." He leaned forward and kissed her on the forehead.

"Morning." She instinctively relaxed. The kind gesture was enough to put Kate at ease, and she sat down beside Lucy.

Suddenly Emma appeared. "Morning all, tuck in," she instructed, before taking up the empty chair beside Kate.

The centre of the table was filled with breakfast goodies. Eggs, bacon, sausages, biscuits and gravy were first choice for the ranch hands, while Jake and Lucy started with pancakes. Kate tucked into fresh fruit and yogurt before helping herself to a bowl of cereal.

Emma checked to see that everyone had what they needed before turning her attention to Kate. "Morning, dear. How did you sleep?"

"Oh, like a log – it's so quiet out here."

"Yes, yes it is, apart from at meal times," Emma chuckled. "And how are you two today? All ready for school?"

Jake and Lucy had their mouths full, but they both nodded politely.

"Good. Oh, that reminds me." Emma got to her feet again and disappeared to the far side of the kitchen.

A few minutes later she returned with two plastic containers, one yellow, one green, and placed them in front of Jake and Lucy. "Take your pick of the colours, they're both the same inside."

"Yellow please," Lucy declared, a little louder than Kate would have liked.

"That means you're green then, Jake." Jake seemed quite happy with that.

"You, you made them a lunch?" Kate asked, her surprise evident in her tone.

"Yes, dear. Oh – is that not alright?"

"Oh yes, yes, of course, it's just, well, it's just so kind of you. So thoughtful. I really didn't expect you to go to the trouble."

"It's no trouble, dear, no trouble at all. And when you have a minute, I should show you where things are in the kitchen in case you want a coffee or something to eat when I'm not around."

"Thank you, Emma, I would really appreciate that."

Kate looked across at Matthew. He winked at her and gave her a little smile as if to say 'I told you so'. She just laughed at him and hurried her children up. There was a feast on the table and they would sit and work their way through it if left.

"Okay, children, almost time to go. What do you say to Emma?"

"Thank you, Emma," they said, grabbing their lunchboxes and leaving the table.

"Now go wipe your faces."

To Emma's surprise, Lucy ran back to give her a hug. "Oh! Bye, dear. Have a good day."

Kate sat for a minute to finish her coffee and Matthew moved round to sit beside her.

"Do you have all the information you need for school this morning? Postal address, phone number, mobiles?"

"Yes, it's all in my bag, ready to go."

The table began to empty as the men headed back out to work. John, however, took a seat across from Matthew and Kate. "Thought I'd better come and wish you luck before you step inside the office today, Kate," he teased.

"Surely it can't be that bad," she laughed.

"Don't answer that, Dad, it's a leading question," Matthew joked, giving Kate a wink.

"In all seriousness though, Kate," John stiffened, "I know I don't have the time. We need someone in there, someone we can trust, to keep it going from day to day. Anyway, I hate it." He leaned back in his chair and clasped his hands behind his head. "I want to be outside on the land with the cattle and horses. The planning and forecasting I'm good at but the day-to-day stuff has become far too much now. I know that with Matthew's legal brains and your business brains it's the sensible thing to do." Then, wagging a finger at her playfully, "Just remember I'm still the boss, so any decisions or issues to be discussed are done right here at this table while I'm eating a slice of Emma's cake, understood?"

Matthew laughed and headed out into the hallway to fetch the keys to his truck.

Kate reached across towards John. "Thank you, John, for letting us be here."

John's expression softened; he knew from what little Matthew had told him that she had been through something terrible and although he had no idea what, he could also see it for himself in her demeanour. He was just glad that she was here, and that she was safe. "I've known you for years, Kate. You are family, you know that."

"Look what I found on my way back to the kitchen." Kate and John turned to see Matthew walking in with Lucy dangling under one arm and Jake being wrestled with the other.

The kitchen was filled with laughter and it felt good. John looked at Kate, nodding towards Matthew. "He's single you know."

"Okay, time to go, grab your bags and lunches," Kate instructed, ushering her children out the door whilst at the same time trying to hide her blushes.

Kate and Matthew had their whole day planned out. Firstly, Matthew was going to drive them all into school and Kate was going to run in quickly and update their address and contact details and ask about getting her children on the school bus. Then it was back to the ranch and into the office.

By nine forty-five the school run was over, and they were both standing in the office, mug of coffee in hand, laughing at the amount of work ahead of them. Matthew switched the computer on as Kate began to have a good look around. She began with the large three-door cupboard. There were rows of shallow boxes, the lids from boxes of A4 paper, each filled with paperwork but in no obvious order.

"What are these?" she asked, confused.

"Dad's filing system. Each box represents a month, I think, or is it a company? Maybe both."

Kate had never seen such a waste of space. The shelves were deep enough to hold half a dozen stacked up and yet they were laid out side by side. She continued round and looked at the tiered trays on the bench and then the filing cabinets. There was no obvious system in place, chronological or alphabetical. There was a lot of sorting to be done but Kate was unsure of how much she could change.

"Who does your accounts? Is it you, or does the accountant do everything?" She could see no system for them.

"We give everything to the accountant at the end of our tax year. I've said to Dad that we would save a fortune doing them in-house, but we don't have the time or the knowledge to do it properly."

"I do. You should have far more of a handle on that side of things in here. It would also allow you to look forward more accurately when budgeting."

Matthew had started a list; he had called it 'Kate's Orders'.

"Ha ha, you're funny."

"Okay, computer's up," he said, walking over and picking up his dad's chair for Kate.

She sat beside him and waited as he opened Excel. He took her through all the new records and budgets he had created as well as the new folders. She had also taken to adding to the Kate's Orders list. Everything Matthew had done made sense and he knew Excel inside out. She would never have managed to create the formulas and sums to make them work to the extent he had but now that they had been created she would be able to use them. She could look at the figures and information they spat out and know exactly what to do with them, where to adjust and improve and where to pull back.

A couple of hours later they sat back in their chairs, exhausted from looking at numbers. They chatted and made plans together about how to take things forward and Kate's business knowledge was making Matthew look at things in a whole new light.

At the same time Kate could feel herself buzzing. For the first time in a very long time she was using her brain and the more she delved into things the more it all came rushing back to her. She felt she had a purpose, and could already see where things could be greatly improved. She had already spotted ways of saving the ranch money, although she still had to investigate further to be certain, so she kept that to herself for now. But she felt alive, she felt needed and she felt an overwhelming urge to hug Matthew. She threw her arms around him and kissed him on the cheek, not a peck but a lingering kiss.

"What was that for?" he asked, his blue eyes looking straight into hers.

"I…I don't know." She blushed. "I just, I…"

Matthew laughed and pulled her towards him.

"That's alright, you can hug and kiss me any time you like, and for the record, it doesn't have to be just on the cheek."

Still blushing, Kate shuffled in her chair.

He nudged her teasingly with his elbow. "Come on, it's almost lunchtime and we deserve a break."

As she followed him out the door, she was grateful to him for changing the subject but at the same time, she had no idea of the impact that moment had had on Matthew. For the first time she was the one who had made a physical move. It had been spontaneous and carefree and confirmed to Matthew that there was hope. Hope that one day she might be able to move on from the damage Adam had done. To Matthew, Kate would always be worth the wait.

There was the usual gathering for lunch. A crowded table full of humour and genuine niceness with a chunk of mickey-taking thrown in. Kate looked at the two empty chairs. She always missed her children when they were at school, but today, for the first time since they started school in Colorado Springs, she wasn't feeling isolated and alone.

After a quick lunch Kate and Matthew were back in

the office. The afternoon was spent looking through the filing cabinets, desks, cupboards and tiered trays, which Kate decided were no longer fit for the purpose given. She could think of better ways to use them.

There were files and boxes with paperwork dating back years. Some important, some not and some with brochures for companies that no longer existed. There was also a mountain of paperwork that could be archived, giving them much-needed space for ring-binders and box files. They sat together creating a plan. Whatever system was put in place they both had to understand it. Matthew decided he would take the mornings off the ranch for the rest of the week and work with Kate in the office. She would then carry on with what they had discussed in the afternoons while he worked out on the ranch. Hopefully by the end of the week they would know where everything was and what everything was for, allowing Kate to start looking into how she could take things forward from the next week. They also pencilled in time on Friday morning to explain their findings to John.

Suddenly Kate came out of her thoughts. “The kids – what time is it?”

“It’s okay, we still have half an hour.”

Kate buried her face in her hands. She had become so engrossed in the office, so engrossed in doing something she loved, but the fact she had completely forgotten to keep an eye on the time horrified her. “I will need to make sure I remember tomorrow,” she said, throwing some papers back into a box the same way she had found them, sideways and upside down.

"Wait, how will I get them if you're out on the ranch?"

"What do you mean?"

"Well how will I get there? Is there a bus?"

Matthew laughed. "You'll take the truck, will you not?"

"The truck?" she exclaimed, a little louder than intended.

"Yes, or one of the ranch vehicles if mine isn't about."

Matthew lifted his head from the file he was trying to decipher. "Kate, you live here, you work here. If you ever need to go anywhere you just take one of the trucks, no questions asked. Mine if it's about, it's much cleaner inside, but any of them. I will get you on the insurance when we come back from picking the kids up today and this evening I will show you properly around Colorado Springs. Routes to places other than the school, to get you used to driving again." His dark blue eyes were looking straight into hers. His matter-of-fact tone was laced with kindness and this was something she was still struggling to get used to. In the past such matter-of-fact statements would have been loaded with threats and intimidations and would certainly have been full of commands that had to be obeyed.

She kept his gaze as she stepped closer. "You're a good man, Mr Harrison, and I have absolutely no idea what I have done to deserve you in my life."

"Are you going to kiss me again?"

14

It was now Friday, and Kate sat alone at the large dining table. The breakfast dishes had been cleared away and Emma had gone into town for groceries. She looked around the empty room. It was one of her favourite rooms in the house, still warm and inviting even when no one else was around. She thought about the once dreaded mealtimes and how much she loved them now. She found herself looking forward to them, joining in conversations up and down the table. She was getting to know the ranch hands, getting to know their different personalities, and was joining in with their banter. Jake and Lucy were also thriving; they were enjoying being part of something much bigger. The younger ranch hands seemed to enjoy including them when they could, often kicking a ball around with Jake after dinner. Although Kate suspected that Matthew might have had something to do with that.

She was brought from her thoughts as a veranda door swung open and Matthew and John appeared, ready for their Friday meeting. Matthew leaned across and kissed Kate on the forehead before going to wash his hands.

"There had better be cake, you promised cake," John said, glancing at a table laid out only with paperwork.

Kate rose from her chair and headed towards the kitchen. She filled three mugs with coffee from the percolator and added cream and sugar. She was getting to know how everyone took their coffee, even the ranch hands, and Kate liked that.

She set the coffee down in front of Matthew and John before returning to the kitchen to collect one of Emma's delicious homemade carrot cakes and three plates.

"You really have cake?" Matthew gasped in delight as he took a plate.

"Yeah, I figured a certain someone might stay a little longer if there was cake," she chuckled, glancing across at John as she took her seat beside Matthew.

"Well, I will stay as long as you like now."

They sat for almost three hours going over Kate's notes. They discussed her findings on how to simplify the office and get it running more efficiently. She suggested changes to how the books were kept, what was and was not recorded, and how to simplify and update the filing system. She also asked John about the accounts. She knew she could save them a fortune if she took on the day-to-day running of the books, leaving the accountant with only the complicated end-of-year stuff. She questioned them on why they ordered from certain wholesalers every eight weeks when leaving it to every twelve would mean ordering larger quantities, resulting in bigger discounts and in some cases waving delivery fees. She noted that they used numerous wholesalers for different items, but one or two wholesalers stocked all the items. If they only ordered from one or two places their discount would again be bigger, and the delivery costs would go completely.

Matthew and John could see that what Kate was suggesting would not only save them a small fortune, but it would streamline the running of the office as well. What Kate didn't appreciate was the impact this would also have out on the ranch. One or two deliveries coming in was far less time-consuming than half a dozen. John was delighted. He knew Kate would be a real asset to the business side of the ranch and more importantly he knew he could trust her completely.

"How do you feel about all that, Kate?" John asked. "It would mean you taking on far more than we had originally discussed."

"To be honest, I'm more than happy. It feels great to have a purpose and to be using my brain again."

"Right, perfect. Let's get the wheels in motion," John replied, rubbing his hands together before reaching over to cut another slice of cake.

"You would need to talk to your accountant though, come to an agreement about what we did here and how they wanted things presented at the year end," Kate added.

"Okay, well you and Matthew do that. There's no point in me being involved in that, not now," John replied.

"Also, would you mind if I ordered some stationery – files and folders? Actually, a hole punch would be great." She couldn't help but chuckle.

Matthew smiled. "Yes, whatever you need. Can I be there when you do that? There are some things I could do with ordering too."

"Of course. And I have one other suggestion. Something for you both to mull over. The three abandoned bunkhouses down beyond the cattle sheds."

Matthew and John looked at each other instinctively and grinned.

"What, what are you both grinning at?"

"They'd make perfect holiday homes, wouldn't they," Matthew replied.

"Yes, yes they would."

Matthew turned to his dad. "See, I told you."

Kate laughed. "Okay, I will leave you both to mull that one over. I'm going into town after lunch to get my hair cut then I'm meeting Maggie for coffee. Will you manage if I transfer calls to your mobiles?"

"Yes, that's fine," Matthew replied, handing her the keys to his truck.

They could hear Emma scuttling about in the kitchen, back from her grocery shopping, and John rose from the table, taking his empty plate with him. "Better get this cleared away for lunch."

Matthew and Kate gathered up the paperwork from the table and headed towards the office.

"It looks better in here already," Matthew commented, as he put the paperwork on Kate's desk.

"It won't when the folders arrive," she laughed. "Everything will get emptied and sorted through properly then."

Kate walked over to her desk and looked out the window. John was outside talking to Blake and Owen. "Do you think your dad is okay with all this? I mean, the office has ended up getting a complete overhaul."

Matthew joined her and sat back against the corner of her desk. "He's fine, honestly. The place needed it and to be honest I think he's enjoying putting all his energy into outside. He's also got his evenings back. Trust me, he's a happy man. I would say if he wasn't. How about you though, are you happy?"

Kate gave a chuckle as she turned to face Matthew. "I'm loving it. I can see how the office will run once everything has been sorted out and I'm looking forward to seeing what money I can save on the orders. What about you, Mr Harrison, are you happy?"

"Happy?" Matthew exclaimed. He stood up and pulled her closer. "If you don't know the answer to that then there is something seriously wrong with you."

He looked at her. At her hair, her eyes, her mouth. He wanted to kiss her right there and then, and not on the forehead as he always did. He lowered his gaze down to her lips, slightly blushed from her lipstick, and back up to her dark eyes. He was trying to decide if it was the right time, whether

Kate was ready, when she leaned forward and brushed her lips against him. Half on his cheek, half on his mouth. She lingered for a moment before tucking her head into his neck and holding him tight.

Kate and Matthew had held each other often but this time it was different. He could feel her skin, her lips, her breath on his neck; her whole body had given in to the embrace. Matthew brought his hand up to the nape of her neck and cradled her head before running his fingers down through her long wavy hair.

The sound of the ranch hands coming in for lunch brought them out of their embrace. Matthew took Kate's hand in his and brought it up to his lips. He kissed her gently on her palm before clasping it tightly and leading her towards the kitchen for lunch.

15

Kate was running slightly late as she drove into Colorado Springs. She took a shortcut and somehow managed to get to the hair salon in time. As she sat waiting for her stylist she realised that she had become quite good at getting herself around town. She knew the shortcuts, the best places to park and the congested streets to avoid.

It brought back memories of her journey from New York to Colorado Springs, when she had looked out from the many buses and had almost envied the women and children rushing around, getting on with their lives. She remembered wondering if her life would ever be like that again where she was rushing around freely, happily getting on with her life. If only she could have glimpsed a short way into the future and seen her life as it was now. A happy life with her children and the man she adored.

She thought about Matthew and about the moment they had shared in the office just before lunch. That man has put his life on hold for me, she realised. He is waiting for me, waiting for me to be ready.

Kate knew she was getting better; after all, she had made the move today. Kissing Matthew, almost on the mouth, was a huge step forward and she couldn't deny the fire she felt inside each time they touched each other. However, the thought of being physical with someone was hard. She had forgotten the pleasure it brought. She'd had years of painful taking and that was the hurdle she was struggling to get over. She was terrified that being intimate with another man, no matter how gentle, would bring back the memories she had fought so hard to block out.

"Kate!" Her stylist, mid-twenties and sporting a short pink haircut, brought her from her thoughts. She stood and followed the stylist towards the back of the salon.

Meanwhile, John and Matthew were down at the stables with Jesse, Blake and Owen. They had cattle to move that afternoon and Matthew watched his dad as he gave the men their instructions. He had a great respect for his dad. Yes, he was getting older and had struggled to keep up in the office, but that was purely down to the advancement of technology and the increasing workload of the thriving ranch. He knew his father knew ranching inside out and was a fountain of knowledge. He was a man of integrity and deserved the respect his ranch hands had for him. Matthew knew if he was half the man his father was then he would be doing alright. The two men worked together daily, each as happy as the other to be working together.

Matthew's thoughts were interrupted by ringing from his pocket. He pulled out his mobile phone and answered. John watched his son's face as he walked around the cattle yard – his expression had changed. Matthew had become concerned.

"I'll be right there." Matthew glanced back at his dad as he ran towards his dad's truck. "I have to go, Jake's got himself upset over something at school."

Thirty minutes later Matthew was running up the steps to the school entrance. He pressed the buzzer. "Matthew Harrison," he said quickly, before pulling the door towards him. As he walked up to reception the lady behind the desk was already alerting Mr Saunders to his arrival.

Mr Saunders exited a blue door opposite. "Mr Harrison," he greeted, walking across to shake Matthew's hand.

"Yes, what's happened?"

"Jake got himself quite upset this afternoon about the treatment a fellow classmate was getting from another pupil. Jake hasn't done anything wrong. It's what he has gotten himself so upset about that has concerned me. The other boy was bullying his classmate verbally. Calling him names, talking him down and trying to control who he played with. Jake is friendly with this boy and I know he was only defending him, but he is very young to have picked up on such a specific form of bullying. When I spoke to him about why he was so upset he mentioned his dad and it got deeper than I cared to take it without someone from home being here."

"Where is Jake now?"

"In my office." Mr Saunders gestured towards the open blue door.

Matthew walked straight across the hallway and into the office. "Jake."

Jake was sitting in a chair at Mr Saunders' desk. His eyes were swollen from crying, but he perked up at the sight of Matthew.

"It's alright," Matthew said, putting a reassuring hand on Jake's shoulder.

Mr Saunders walked round his desk and sat down. "Please do take a seat, Mr Harrison," he instructed, pointing towards the empty chair beside Jake.

"No," Matthew replied firmly. Both Jake and Mr Saunders looked at him, quite taken aback at Matthew's sharp response. "Jake hasn't mentioned his dad in weeks and if he does decide to open up about him today I would rather he did it at home, with Kate and the rest of his family around him. Not here."

Mr Saunders nodded. "Quite right, Mr Harrison."

"I'll take Jake with me now if that's okay. But can I talk to Lucy? She hasn't been getting the school bus long and I would like to check she's alright about getting on without Jake."

"Certainly, follow me."

Matthew lifted Jake's school bag and with a gentle smile

nodded for him to follow. The three of them walked silently down the corridor until Mr Saunders eventually stopped outside a door. He knocked and walked in. Matthew could hear him. "Can I see Lucy for a moment please, Mrs Walker?"

Lucy walked out into the corridor with Mr Saunders. "Matthew!" she exclaimed, bursting into a run and wrapping her arms around his legs.

Matthew crouched down and moved her hair away from her eyes.

"Lucy, Jake isn't feeling very well so I'm going to take him home. Will you be okay getting on the bus yourself after school? I'll be waiting for you at the end of the driveway when you get off."

Lucy nodded and smiled. He gave her a hug. "That's a girl. I'll see you soon. You better get back into class, you might be missing something important." As she walked in Mr Saunders followed and Matthew could hear him telling Mrs Walker that Lucy would be getting on the bus alone today.

Mr Saunders walked Matthew and Jake back up the corridor towards the door. As he opened it he thanked Matthew for coming in so quickly and told Jake he would look forward to seeing him in school tomorrow. Jake and Matthew started to walk down the steps.

"Mr Harrison?"

Matthew stopped and glanced back. Mr Saunders gave him a nod – he was no longer concerned about Jake. Matthew nodded back and continued down the steps. As they neared the bottom Jake slipped his hand into Matthew's. Matthew made no fuss, he simply held it until they reached the truck.

Matthew opened the back door and Jake jumped in.

"Okay, so we have about an hour to spare before your sister gets on the bus. Your mum is at the hairdressers and meeting Maggie. So how about an ice cream?"

Jake's face lit up. He had wondered if he was in trouble, so the offer of ice cream assured him he was off the hook.

"I will take that smile as a yes," Matthew said, turning the truck in the direction of the diner.

Matthew managed to park right outside the door. As Jake headed for their usual table Tina walked across to take their order.

"Okay, so what will it be today?"

Matthew nodded to Jake to order first.

"Can I have cookie-dough ice cream please?"

"Sounds perfect. Make that two please, Tina."

Tina wandered off to prepare their order.

"Well, I have to say, it's changed a bit since I was last in the principal's office."

Jake's eyes widened. "You were called to the principal's office?"

"Quite often when I was very young, I'm ashamed to say." Matthew raised an eyebrow mischievously.

"Why, what did you do?"

"Silly things, but when I started school I felt a little different to everyone else."

"Why?" Jake was hanging on Matthew's every word.

"My mum died when I was very little, before I started

school, and I just felt different to everyone around me. I was lucky though, I had Emma. She was very young back then and wasn't long married to Jesse. She, well, she was always there for me. She made sure I was alright, that I had everything I needed, that I mixed with other children. Very soon I realised that my situation may well have been different but that I was actually very lucky. I had an amazing family around me and I was well taken care of. That was the important thing. The now was the important thing, not the pain and upset from the past. After that I was never called in to the principal's office again unless it was for something good. Anyway," he said, changing his tone to lighten the mood, "thank goodness they've painted it. It used to be pale green, always reminded me of vomit."

"Here we go, two cookie-dough ice creams."

Jake watched in admiration as Matthew thanked Tina. In his own little way, Jake was just as taken aback as Kate by people showing others kindness.

"Tuck in," Matthew gestured. "We must be back before your mum gets home. She doesn't know you won't be on the bus."

An hour later Matthew was parking the truck at the entrance to Wester Lakes. "Come on, I want to show you something."

Jake and Matthew jumped from the truck and Matthew nodded towards one of the stone walls that sat at either side of the entrance to the driveway. One side had a big wooden name plaque, but Matthew and Jake went and stood with their backs leaning against the other. They looked out at the vast expanse of the ranch. Matthew pointed out the different landmarks. He showed Jake where their land started and stopped and told him about his favourite parts of the ranch. He also told him about the forestry side and the long-term nature of the ranch. As the two of them chatted they were forming a bond, a bond far stronger than Matthew had ever hoped.

Jake had seen Matthew in a completely different light this afternoon. He had watched as Matthew had dealt with the situation at school firmly but politely, stood up for Jake and made sure Lucy was okay. Matthew had opened Jake's eyes to a different world. A world a million miles away from the life he had known in New York. Jake knew everyone at Wester Lakes was friendly and kind. He knew Matthew and his mum had known each other for a long time but he was only now realising that everyone at Wester Lakes truly cared about them, that they looked on them as family, and it was a moment in Jake's life that he would never forget.

"Oh, I hear wheels," Matthew said, turning to see Kate driving into Wester Lakes. She smiled at Matthew, but her smile turned to concern when she spotted Jake standing beside him. She parked and jumped from the truck.

"It's okay," Matthew reassured her as she rushed across to her son.

"Hi, Mum, we've just had ice cream."

Kate looked at Matthew confused.

"Why don't you two go for a walk and a chat while I wait for Lucy, maybe down the path by the trees?" he suggested. "No ears there."

Kate nodded; she realised this was a conversation to be had in private.

"It's okay," Matthew reassured again as she ushered Jake towards her truck.

When Kate and Jake returned from their walk they found Matthew sitting at the dining table with Lucy. She was doing her homework and he was listening to her reading.

"Jake, would you sit with Lucy for a minute please while I talk to Matthew?"

As Matthew rose from the table Kate took him by the hand and led him down the hallway and into the office, closing the door behind them.

"Jake told me what you did, what you said, how you made sure Lucy was okay, about your chat at the diner. You sorted everything out in his little head for him without him having to say a word. It's the most fatherly thing anyone has ever done for him, Matthew, and he knows it."

"What else was I going to do. I care about him, Kate, he's a great kid. They both are."

"Vomit green, huh?"

"Yeah, but it let me get a point across. And by the way, tomorrow we are buying you a mobile phone."

She leaned towards him. "I've said it before and I'll say it again. You're a good man, Mr Harrison." Smiling, she kissed him on the cheek.

"And I've said it before and I'll say it again. It doesn't always have to be the cheek," he flirted.

She looked up into his deep blue eyes and down at his

lips, just as he had done to her earlier that day. She lifted her gaze back up to his eyes. She knew he would never make the first move, he respected her too much. She could smell him, feel his breath on her face, and the urge to kiss him was all-consuming. She looked back down at his lips and, leaning in further, she kissed him.

Matthew was hesitant at first. Was it a peck? Was he even to take part? He didn't want to rush her. But Kate pushed her whole body into his and they both fell into a long, deep kiss. It was hard and passionate to start before settling into a loving, gentle, arousing kiss.

Kate felt Matthew on her hip and stepped back. She didn't want to lead him on and she knew she wasn't ready to take things further.

"It's okay, it's okay," he said quietly, pulling her back and wrapping his arms around her. "In your time, Kate, in your time."

Leaning in, she kissed him again just as passionately before pulling away. "I'd better go and check on the children."

"I'm going to need a minute," Matthew replied, slightly embarrassed as she left the room.

He glanced out the window. His dad had parked the truck outside. Wondering how long he had been there he watched as his dad came into the ranch house and headed upstairs. A few moments later Matthew followed. His dad had gone into his den, just as he did every evening before dinner.

"Everything alright with Jake this afternoon, son?"

"Yeah... Maybe I need to tell you a little more about what the kids have been through, Dad."

John sank into a sofa and signalled to Matthew to join him. "Just the kids?"

Matthew sat opposite his dad. "Kate's been through far worse than Jake and Lucy, Dad. It's not my place to tell you, I can't."

"Okay, well a little about the kids would help, just so I understand."

Matthew told his dad about Jake's reaction at school earlier that day and as much as he felt he could about their life back in New York with Adam. John sat forward. He was very fond of Kate, he always had been, and he was becoming very fond of her children too. The thought of them suffering was hard for John to take. "Oh, Matthew. That's..." he trailed off, not knowing what to say.

"I know," Matthew said, knowing exactly how his dad felt.

"And what about you, son?"

"What about me?"

"I parked the truck at the wrong time this evening. I saw you and Kate in the office. I have to say I'm delighted things are moving along there. It's about time."

"We are moving along but at a pace Kate can cope with."

John looked puzzled; he didn't understand.

"Kate's scars go far deeper than the kids', Dad."

"What do you mean?"

"Adam has hurt Kate in a way that's far worse than you could imagine. It's probably better that you don't know. But,

but…" Matthew looked down at the floor for a few moments before lifting his head again. "I love her, Dad, and when we are together she is the old Kate. The one Adam didn't damage. The one I knew in New York."

"And what about you, son, how long do you wait? What are you missing out on while you wait for something that might never happen?"

"It will, Dad, I know it will. I see it in her eyes every day, the way she looks at me, and I felt it in the office today. We have a connection, a deep connection. We are a couple in our own way. She just needs time to heal."

John sat back and nodded. "Okay, son, okay, but I don't want you getting hurt either. You played the father's role this afternoon. It's a role you're falling into quite naturally and I'm proud of you for that but at the same time be careful."

"She kissed me today, Dad. *She* kissed *me*. Not the other way around."

16

Everyone had gathered round the table for dinner and Kate was helping Emma bring the last of the food across from the kitchen. John, who was in his usual spot at the head of the table, watched as Kate and her children laughed and chatted to the ranch hands as though they had always been part of the household. His head was still reeling from his chat with Matthew earlier that evening, but everything was starting to make sense to him. Kate and her children had appeared from nowhere with nothing other than a couple of kid-sized rucksacks and a few bags. Kate had been subdued when she had first arrived at the ranch but even in the short time they had been there John could see new life being breathed back into her. He was proud of Kate for being brave enough to get herself and her children away from Adam. Without thinking he stood. "Before we start."

Jake and Lucy looked at each other in horror; they were starving and ready to tuck into dinner. Matthew watched his dad; he had no idea what he was about to say.

"Matthew, Kate and I had a meeting this morning about the ranch and my office skills. Although, the least said about those the better." Laughter enveloped the table. "I just wanted to say, Kate, Jake, Lucy, I am delighted you have ended up at our table. You have breathed new life into this house, and, Jake, Lucy, I rather look forward to our evening trips out to check the cattle. So, here's to you and everyone who sits round our happy table." John went to sit down again but stopped. "Oh, and Kate, Matthew, I just got off the phone with the accountant. You have an appointment at nine-thirty on Thursday morning and he also agrees with you both about the old bunkhouses. So, I'm leaving all that to you two."

Kate and Matthew looked at each other as everyone tucked into Emma's delicious dinner. They both knew that renovating the bunkhouses would give them a project to work on together from start to finish and that excited them both.

Kate watched as Matthew instinctively saw to Jake first, making sure he had helped himself to whatever he wanted and reminding him to take some vegetables. Kate thought about John's little speech. She realised she was becoming part of something much bigger than Wester Lakes. She was becoming part of the family. She and her children.

When dinner was over Kate helped Emma tidy up. John, Matthew and the ranch hands went back out to work, and Lucy and Jake finished their homework.

When John and Matthew returned Kate was sitting at the table, sipping coffee and chatting to her children. John was collecting Lucy and Jake for their evening drive to check the cattle and Matthew was heading back out. He had just received a call from Owen to say that one of their horses was lame.

Kate found herself sitting in silence in the empty kitchen. It was peaceful. She thought about the day they had all had. It had been eventful to say the least. She thought about her morning in the office with Matthew and again in the afternoon when she had kissed him. She had no regrets. She had been longing to kiss him since that first day in the diner, but now what? Where did that leave them? She wanted a full relationship with Matthew more than anything but whenever she thought about them getting intimate she saw Adam's face and the memories of what he did to her and how she felt at the time came flooding back. She could feel tears welling up in her eyes again. She had cried so often in the last few weeks and months and she was getting fed up. Fed up of tears. Fed up of how Adam was still affecting her life. Fed up of her own inability to move on.

She was so lost in her thoughts that she hadn't heard Emma come back into the kitchen.

"Are you alright, dear? Sorry, I didn't mean to startle you." Emma had noticed Kate's tears as soon as she had walked in. She grabbed herself a mug of coffee and pulled out a chair across from Kate. "A penny for them?"

Kate looked at Emma, confused.

"Your thoughts, dear. A penny for your thoughts."

"Oh," Kate laughed, "I would give you a million pennies if you could make my thoughts go away."

Emma was confused, but she did have some idea of Kate's situation. Emma had known Maggie for years and although Emma knew no details, she did know that Kate and her children had left New York in a hurry. Emma decided to keep it light. If Kate wanted to talk she could but Emma wouldn't push.

"You all seem to have settled in well and it's lovely having young ones in the house."

"Oh, they love it here."

"And what about you, dear? Why the tears?" Emma instantly regretted her question. So much for keeping it light, she thought to herself.

"I love it here too. Matthew, John, you, everyone has been so welcoming."

"So what's the but then?" Emma asked. "I have no idea what is in your past, but I can see what's in your future and he's tall and handsome." She chuckled.

"But what if it's what's in your past that is preventing you from moving forward?" Kate sniffled through more tears.

"I don't understand, dear. Can you not blot it out? What's done is done and move on sort of thing. Have a fresh start."

Kate shot Emma a look.

"Oh, I've said something wrong, I'm sorry, dear." Emma looked flustered.

"No. No," Kate reassured. "You're right, that is exactly what I have to do. I just have to figure out how, that's all." Emma's matter-of-fact perspective was exactly what Kate needed.

Emma was beginning to realise that Kate and her children may have been through far worse than she had realised. "Give it time, dear, whatever it is. Time is a great healer and so is this place." She looked around. "There is something about this ranch. I am always at peace here." Emma rose from the table. "I had better get supper on. The men will be back soon."

Kate followed Emma into the kitchen. The two women worked together to put supper on the table, finishing just in time for the doors to swing open and Jake and Lucy to come running in, followed by a crowd of hungry ranch hands.

Supper over, Kate took Jake and Lucy for their showers. She set their clothes out for the following morning and made sure their school bags had everything they needed.

Once showered they brushed their teeth and ran back up to the kitchen to say goodnight to Matthew and John. Soon they were tucked up in bed and Kate was sitting in her room reading a book. She loved her evenings on her sofa with the veranda door open. It was her own quiet time and she would look up at the mountains behind and feel as though she was part of them.

Tonight, though, was different. She found herself reading the same line over and over. She couldn't get Emma's comments out of her head. *Just blot it out.* Her manner was so decisive. Obviously, Emma had no idea what Kate was trying to blot out, but if Kate couldn't move on Adam had won. Maybe Kate had to take things one step at a time, quite literally.

She got up and tiptoed out into the hallway, popping her head first into Lucy's room and then into Jake's. They were both sound asleep. Kate returned to her room. She stood for a few minutes chewing on her bottom lip and wondering if she had gone truly insane. Then walking across to a chest of drawers she pulled out a lilac satin night slip and held it up against her. She took a deep breath and quickly gathered her hair, clipping it up on top of her head.

Ten minutes later she'd had a quick shower and was undoing the clip. She brushed her hair, put on the satin slip and a little light lipstick. Her slip stopped midway up her thighs. She was a bit worried about the plunging neckline, but it was all she had so it would have to do.

Wrapping her robe around her she quietly tiptoed back out into the hallway and up the stairs. She knocked on Matthew's door but there was no answer. She knew if he was in bed he wouldn't hear so she turned the handle and tiptoed in. She crossed his living-room area towards the door to his bedroom; it was slightly ajar. Taking a deep breath Kate knocked again.

"Come in."

Kate walked in slowly. Matthew was sitting up in bed reading. His bare muscular chest was in full view and her eyes were drawn to his strong shoulders and arms. Her heart beat faster. She tried not to stare.

"Are you okay?" he asked with that bloody smile.

"I wondered if I could lie with you for a little while?" she replied shyly, not quite managing to look him in the eye.

Matthew put his book on his nightstand and pulled the duvet back, signalling to her to get in. He pulled it back just far enough for her to see he was wearing shorts. She was relieved; one thing at a time, she kept telling herself as she removed her robe and stepped closer to the bed.

Matthew watched. She was a vision. Her breasts were being held in by a slither of lilac lace and her slip was clinging to her curves. She sat on the edge of the bed and swung her long, toned slender legs up and under the duvet. He was all too aware of Kate's body; it had barely changed in the years since they had dated back in New York. He remembered their passion, their intimacy, and he so desperately yearned to share it with her again.

"I thought, one step at a time," she said, finally managing to look him in the eye.

"One step at a time," he agreed, turning to switch the bedside lamp off.

He slid further down the bed and pulled the duvet back up over Kate. She slid down beside him. He brought his knees up and slid them in behind hers. Wrapping his strong arm around her he kissed the back of her shoulder as she took his hand in hers.

The feel of her satin slip against his bare chest, the scent from her hair, the feel of her warm smooth skin against his was intoxicating.

She could feel him, his strong sensual body wrapped around hers. She felt safe, safer than she had ever felt.

*

The early morning light cast a glow across the bedroom. Matthew stirred. He was lying on his back with his arms around Kate, her head resting on his chest and her leg draped across his, her arm across his torso, her hand hugging his waist.

He looked down at her face, her lips, her neck. His gaze lowered. Her breasts were pressed into his side, her cleavage barely staying in her slip. His hunger for Kate was as strong as ever and more than anything he wanted to roll her onto her back and make love to her.

Instead, he turned and looked at the clock. It was just after five.

"Kate, Kate." He ran his fingers gently over her forehead, moving her hair away from her face before trailing them down her cheeks and across her lips.

She began to stir, slowly opening her eyes.

"It's just gone five."

"Oh no! I'd better get downstairs," she gasped.

"Dad's alarm goes off at five-thirty, what about the kids'?"

"Mine goes off at six and I wake them."

"Well, I reckon we still have fifteen minutes."

Kate tightened her grip on him and moved her leg further up his. They held each other close before she sneaked out of his room as quietly as she had snuck in.

17

It was half past midnight in New York and Adam was once again pacing the kitchen floor as he attempted to walk off another night's rage. This was something he had done every night since the day Kate had left. He had developed a rigid daily routine which he had not once allowed himself to break.

His days were always the same. Waking to the sound of his alarm at six-thirty he would get up and open his closet. He would take out his freshly pressed shirt and pants, still in their laundered packaging, and hang them beside his mirror. After a quick shower he would get dressed; he needed to be ready to leave at a moment's notice. He always stopped to have a check of himself in the mirror, his immaculate appearance giving the impression of a wealthy and successful family man.

He would then go to the living room to switch on his

laptop before heading to the kitchen to prepare his breakfast. Once he had eaten he would return to his laptop and make his first search of the day. He would type 'Kate Thomas' into the search engine and each morning it would spit out the same results.

He had discovered there were many Kate Thomases spread across the globe and Adam knew everything he possibly could about every single one of them. None of them, however, belonged to him. None of them were his Kate.

Search completed and laptop switched off, he would return to his closet and pull out his immaculate overcoat. Once on he would have a final check of himself in the mirror before picking up his briefcase and heading out the door to work. His head was always down; he hadn't spoken to a single neighbour since the day Kate and the children had left. He knew they would have noticed their absence, but he hadn't admitted to anyone that they had gone, and he had no intention of ever doing so. He would find Kate and bring her back and all would be as it should.

As he entered the main reception of his office building he would say a pleasant good morning to everyone he passed. As he approached his office, colleagues who knew him well would say, "Good morning, Adam, how are Kate and the children?"

"They're great thanks," was always his reply, followed by some little anecdote that he made up about what one of the children had said or done before politely asking about their family. At lunchtime he was always heard on his phone. He would ask Kate how she was and how her morning had been. Did she need any groceries on the way home? His apartment answerphone was always flashing red when he returned home and that day's conversation to Kate was promptly deleted. He would continue with his day's work and leave the office just as immaculately and politely as he had arrived.

Once home for the evening, however, his immaculate demeanour would disappear the moment he stepped inside his apartment. His first task was always to delete his lunchtime message to Kate before switching on his laptop. Then it was straight to his bedroom where his coat would be hung perfectly in his closet ready for the next day, and his pants and shirt thrown into a pile in the corner. Dressed only in his boxers and undershirt he would return to the living room and type 'Kate Thomas' into the search engine again. He would do this repeatedly every thirty minutes without fail. He would sit counting down on his watch, willing the last few seconds to pass to allow him to make the next search. His evenings had become dissected into thirty-minute intervals.

Takeout meals were delivered every evening at five minutes past eight without fail. This allowed him to finish his eight o'clock search with enough time to eat before he began his eight-thirty search. The companies making the deliveries had learned never to be early and, more importantly, never to be late.

As midnight struck and another day passed without any trace of Kate his temper would become all-consuming. His rage would result in the apartment being trashed, just as it had been the night before that and the night before that. It eventually ended with him pacing the kitchen floor as though walking off his rage.

Once he had calmed down he would trample through the chaos to his bedroom and check the individual items of the suitcase he had purchased the day Kate left. It had been sitting packed and ready to go all this time. A change of clothes, underwear and toiletries were neatly packed together alongside his passport. He was ready. The minute there was the slightest trace of Kate he would be off.

He would eventually go to bed trying to recall every conversation he had ever had with Kate to see if there was any clue as to where she might have gone. His days ended with him eventually falling asleep in the early hours of the morning.

He had never once searched for his children's names. The thought hadn't entered his head. He didn't see them as possessions, not like his Kate. He was convinced he would find her and bring her back. Even if it took him years. He would never give up. She belonged here with him. After all, she was his.

Tomorrow he would get up and do it all over again and the day after that and the day after that and the day after that until he had her back.

18

It had been a couple of weeks since Kate and Matthew had had their appointment with the accountant. The stationery order had arrived, and Kate had spent much of her time filing, sorting, archiving and shredding. The office was now functioning efficiently, and Kate knew exactly how the accounts were to be presented at each year end. She and Matthew had developed a system that was easy to keep on top of and that they both understood. Although John didn't have a clue how Matthew and Kate had got the figures onto the spreadsheets he completely understood them when he sat down and read them. He was delighted that they could put a considered expense into the sheet and instantly see the effect it would have months or years down the line.

Kate's next job was to analyse the invoices sitting for

payment, look at where to order from in the future and get all outstanding invoices paid.

This morning, however, was the start of a brand-new week and as Kate and Matthew waved goodbye to the school bus she slipped her arm around his waist. He turned and kissed her. His kisses were no longer on her forehead and neither cared who saw.

Jumping back into the truck Matthew turned it around and drove them back to the ranch house. John was waiting on the veranda with the keys to the old bunkhouses and he jumped in the back of the truck before Matthew headed off again towards the disused bunkhouses. As they carried on down the track they discussed their concerns about the access to the ranch. If the bunkhouses were renovated and turned into holiday homes, it wouldn't be safe to have guests roaming around a working ranch and their first concern had to be the animals. Matthew had spent the previous week making calls and had been told that they would almost certainly be given permission to reopen an old access road from the bunkhouses to the main road. It had been blocked off years ago with large boulders but could easily be cleared. They would then block off the track from the bunkhouses to the rest of the ranch. Guests would have their own access in and out without having to come onto the ranch.

John unlocked the door of the first bunkhouse and wandered in. Kate followed close behind, keeping her eyes to the floor. She was worried about mice or worse and was relieved to see that the bunkhouse was in a much better state than she had imagined. After inspecting all three they were sure the bulk of the work would be cosmetic. Structurally they were all in good condition. The bathrooms and kitchens would need to be replaced, as would all the baseboards and internal doors, but apart from that it was purely redecoration and furnishings.

Wandering back outside, they sat on the remains of an old stone wall and continued making notes. They knew each bunkhouse would need its own outdoor seating area, perhaps a patio and low-maintenance garden to make them welcoming and homely. The external upkeep would have to be added to the ranch rota though, so they needed to keep the impact there to a minimum.

"Right, we had better head back," John said, rising from the wall. "I'm meeting Jesse at the cattle sheds – we need to check the river levels."

"Okay, Dad, we'll drop you on the way. I'm going to phone a couple of contractors I know, start getting some quotes. The sooner the bunkhouses are finished the sooner we can rent them out. If we have them ready for spring, we'll get a return on them in the summer – if not it would be another year."

"Great, let me know how that goes."

Matthew nodded. "We are also going into town this afternoon. Kate and the kids are needing some warmer clothes for winter coming in and boots for wearing around the ranch."

"Good," John replied before lowering his voice. "Make

sure it all goes on account, the kids too. They more than deserve a little spoiling and Kate has done a lot for us here."

An hour later Matthew was driving them both into town. Kate knew he was right. Neither she nor her children had clothes or footwear suitable for the ranch, winter was coming, and her children were rapidly growing out of the clothes she had bought when they first arrived in Colorado Springs. However, she was quietly concerned. She had no idea where they were going or what the prices would be like and she knew she didn't want to spend too much. The ranch was paying her in cash as she still hadn't opened a bank account, still hadn't given her surname to anyone other than the school, and she was just starting to get on her feet financially. The anxiety she had felt for years about not having any money of her own was gone and she was enjoying being able to plan financially for the first time in years.

Matthew pulled up outside what looked like a giant warehouse that sat on its own about a mile outside of town. Jumping out of the truck they walked towards the entrance hand in hand. Matthew held the door open for Kate as she walked in but she had only taken a few steps when she turned and walked out again. Matthew quickly followed.

"I can't afford this. We'll have to go somewhere else."

"Kate, it's going to be colder here in winter and you all need new clothes. We're out in the ranch in all weathers."

"I know, but I can't afford to kit *me* out in there, never mind the kids too. Please let's just go somewhere else."

"It's all going on account, Kate."

"No, no way, Matthew," she retorted abruptly. "I'm not charity."

"No, no you're not, but you do work on the ranch. The hands get supplies from here too when they need them. Anyway, as far as I'm concerned you are my family and you are all needing new clothes and decent footwear."

Kate hung her head. She knew Matthew was right, but she had her pride. He had given her so much already and she couldn't keep taking.

"Look, you are going to save us a fortune the way you are restructuring our ordering and you are working far more than the few hours we had originally discussed. You are part of the team, Kate. Don't you see that you're one of us and you can't be running around the ranch in those skimpy sneakers. They are barely safe at this time of year, never mind during the winter."

Kate looked down at her feet. She was still wearing the same old pair of sneakers she had worn when she had travelled from New York to Colorado Springs, and to be honest if she never saw them again it would be too soon.

"Okay, but we reduce my salary this month by whatever we spend in here. Deal?"

"No deal."

Kate looked back at him angrily.

"Well, do you want me to lie? Say yes while we're here then pay you the same anyway? Please, Kate, let me get you and the kids sorted out. You'll never get through the winter with what you have now."

Kate knew she had little choice and wasn't going to win this battle. She knew he was right and turned to walk back inside. Matthew grabbed her arm.

"Are we okay?"

"Yes, we're okay. You are just too good to me. I don't expect it and I don't want you thinking I am only hanging around for what you have. I don't want anyone thinking that."

"Come on, Kate, you know I would never think that of you."

"I know. It's just your kindness again and I can't repay you in any way. I have nothing to give you other than me and the kids."

Matthew's tone was now one of raw emotion tinged with exasperation as he took hold of Kate by the shoulders. "Bloody hell, Kate, that's all I want. You and the kids. All I want is you and the kids here with me. If we had met again and I had nothing our connection would still be the same. I know that, and you know that. I walk on eggshells with you too you know."

"What do you mean?"

"I mean I want to take care of you and be a partner to you, but I am terrified that you think I'm trying to control you the way Adam did. I am so aware of how he treated you that I am sometimes unsure of where the line lies between being caring and controlling."

Kate looked up at Matthew. At his blue eyes. At his moment of weakness. Her voice softened. "You can't begin to imagine how Adam treated me. Believe me, you could never be anything like him. You are the kindest man I have ever met. You take no nonsense and you stand your ground but in a caring and protecting way. Never controlling and always with respect. Be yourself and follow your instincts. That is the man I fell in love with." She wrapped her arms around his neck. "I love you, Matthew, with all my heart. I always have."

He held her close, unable to speak and never wanting to let her go.

"Come on, Mr Harrison, I need to get kitted out for the winter," she said, taking his hand and leading him back inside.

Kate looked around at the vast open space. They started with jackets, then jeans and pants, tops, woollens and fleeces. She spotted a couple of long-sleeve T-shirts she thought might be good to layer up with and added them to her pile before heading towards a cubicle. Matthew continued to wander round to pass the time. He spotted a couple of tops he thought she might like and took them across.

As he approached her cubicle, he noticed the black faux-velvet curtains didn't quite meet. He could see Kate; she was putting a top back onto a hanger and wearing nothing but a set of matching purple underwear. To him she was flawless: tall, slim and elegant. He watched as she put her jeans back on and tried on a long-sleeve T-shirt and fleece. He stepped forward.

"Kate."

She pulled the curtain back. "What do you think?" she asked, gesturing towards the fleece. Matthew leaned in, blushing a little.

"I preferred the purple underwear."

Finally, Kate was kitted out. She'd had no idea she needed so much. Gloves, scarves, hats and waterproofs were also added to her pile and a pair of good strong boots for out on the ranch as well as a dressier pair for going into town. They also picked a selection of clothes and footwear for Jake and Lucy, including a pair of riding boots each. They hoped it would all fit but it could be exchanged if it didn't.

Matthew and Kate arrived back at the ranch just in time to watch the school bus drive into the entrance of Wester Lakes. Jake and Lucy came running to greet them. The greeting was now equal. If a passer-by were to be looking on they would have no reason to doubt Matthew was their father.

"Who is up for a ride on Annabel?" Matthew asked as they all climbed into the truck.

"Me!" Their response, as ever, was in unison.

As Matthew drove towards the stables he and Kate listened as Jake and Lucy were full of the stories of their day. Suddenly Lucy remembered she had something very important to ask.

"Mrs Walker has asked us if any of our mums or dads have really exciting jobs. If they did, they could come and talk to the class about it. Matthew, can you come and talk about the ranch, please?"

Matthew looked at Kate. He could feel a lump forming in his throat.

"Will you, will you?" Lucy repeated excitedly. "Please."

"Of course I will. You just say when and I'll be there."

"Yay!" A delighted Lucy sat back in her seat quite content

while an emotional Matthew sat in the driver's seat. Kate took his hand in hers as he drove towards the stables.

A few hours later Jake and Lucy were showered and ready for bed. They had fallen into the habit of having supper with the ranch hands. It was a little later than Kate would have liked but it seemed cruel to deny them such a pleasure.

"I saw you both out on Annabel this afternoon. How was she?" John asked as he sat down in his usual spot at the head of the table.

"Great," Lucy replied before giving the usual detailed account of her entire experience.

"I was thinking it might be time to put Jake on a slightly bigger pony," Matthew said, throwing Jake a cheeky smile.

"What, really, which one?" Jake asked eagerly.

"I was thinking we could put you on Jasper. What do you think, Dad?"

"I think that's a great idea, son. Jasper's got a lovely temperament, Jake, you'll like him."

"Glad you agree. That way we could get you both out riding at the same time and explore the ranch a bit."

Jake's delight was plain for everyone to see and Kate watched as he chatted and laughed with the ranch hands.

"Right, you two, say goodnight to everyone, it's bedtime."

Jake and Lucy finished their milk and said their goodnights. As Kate went to follow them Matthew grabbed her hand and whispered, "Come lie with me tonight."

This had become quite a habit. If Kate felt the kids were sound, she would tiptoe up the stairs to be with Matthew.

They were always loving and tender, but Kate had still not managed to give herself to Matthew completely. She more than appreciated his patience but she knew he was yearning for more.

Kate went to catch up with her children. She found them both in Jake's room. Lucy was full of chatter about Annabel and her new riding boots and Jake was full of chatter about Matthew. He looked up to Matthew and respected him, something he had never done with his own father.

"I'm going upstairs just now to talk to Matthew. We need to chat about what we're doing tomorrow. Will you be okay? John will be in the living room shortly reading his book and I'll come and check on you both soon." They nodded, and Kate settled them into their beds.

She walked back to the kitchen. Matthew and John were still sitting round the table with the ranch hands. They were deep in conversation about the next day's work rota. It was time to vaccinate the calves and start weaning them off their mother's milk.

Matthew watched as Kate grabbed a bottle of wine and two glasses before walking back out into the hallway.

Half an hour later the ranch chat was over, and Matthew was heading upstairs towards his patch of the house. He found Kate sitting on the sofa in front of the fireplace reading her book. Matthew sat beside her while she poured the wine.

"What's the occasion?"

"No occasion, just us."

Matthew wrapped an arm around her shoulder and she

leaned in, enjoying the closeness. They drank their wine and talked into the night. They chatted about Jake and Lucy, and how effortlessly they had settled into life on the ranch. They had both noticed how attached they had become to both Matthew and John. That mattered to Matthew in more ways than he had realised. He had developed a deep affection for both Jake and Lucy and had willingly taken on a fatherly role.

Their chatter turned to John. It was obvious to everyone that he was enjoying spending more time on the ranch. It appeared that distancing himself from the day-to-day running of the office had had a positive impact and Matthew and Kate both knew that he had complete trust in them. They had their weekly catch-ups and no decisions were made without discussing them with him first.

Kate was starting to realise that her living at the ranch was now a two-way street. Yes, it had been her only solution to begin with, but she now knew she was giving back and playing an important part in the working of the ranch. The admin side of the ranch had never been run so efficiently and knowing she was saving them financially made her feel better about the way in which she and her children had arrived. She was now feeling part of Wester Lakes and it felt good.

Matthew sat forward and topped up their glasses before leaning back again and pulling Kate close. She was enjoying the moment and the calmness that had now become her new life.

"I feel I have been here forever. Like New York was in another lifetime. I can't believe I ran here and found you, that you weren't still happily married and living thirteen hundred miles away in San Francisco."

"Never quite happily," Matthew retorted instinctively. "Do you ever think about him?"

"Every day. When I want to get closer to you, he's there. I don't so much think about what he did now, I've managed to stop thinking about that, but I remember how I felt at the time. It must be in my subconscious. When I start to get closer to you I feel it. It's like a tidal wave of fear that wells up from the pit of my stomach."

Matthew held her tight. "Would you consider a divorce?"

Kate sprung up and turned to face him. "Oh, Matthew, that would be the dream. Right now, though, he has no idea where we are. If I started divorce proceedings it would feel like contact. I wouldn't feel safe. I would feel he was back in my life and might possibly find out where we are. That's a risk I'm just not willing to take."

Matthew totally understood why Kate would feel the way she did. She had come a long way since they had first met back in the diner and she was slowly getting closer, more intimate. But they both knew she had a long way to go. "I like that you've come up here, that we've had the whole evening."

"Me too."

"Will you stay?"

Kate kissed his neck and slowly ran her kisses up to his lips. "I didn't bring anything up with me. I only have my purple underwear."

Matthew gave her a cheeky smile. "That's perfect." They left the sofa and walked arm in arm towards his bedroom.

19

It was the end of a big week at Wester Lakes for Matthew and Kate as work had finally begun on the old bunkhouses. Although the plans had been drawn up weeks before, the contractor had been unable to start until after Thanksgiving; now though, it was full steam ahead as carpenters, electricians and plumbers worked around each other.

Kate was now in the habit of checking on the bunkhouses first thing in the morning, just after she had put Jake and Lucy on the school bus. She was happy with their progress although this was the part where everything felt like it was going backwards. Old fixtures were being removed, walls were being bored into to get to the old electricals and plumbing and the bunkhouses looked in a far worse state than they had before the work began. She knew it would be worth it though, she knew they would be a great source of income once they had recouped their initial renovation costs.

As she sat at the kitchen table waiting for Matthew and John to appear for their usual Friday morning meeting Kate was doing something she hadn't done in years: writing Christmas cards! They were just to Maggie and Walter, Matthew, John, everyone at the ranch and a few contacts she had made since moving to Colorado Springs, but she was still finding it exciting. She longed to send one to Alice, to tell her life was good and that she and her children were safe and happy, but she daren't.

For the first time in years Kate was excited about Christmas; excited about having a tree, excited about having a Christmas dinner, excited about the atmosphere and cheer that would come with it. She hadn't had a proper Christmas since she was a teenager, as her parents had passed away in a car accident. And, once married, Adam wasn't for anything that he couldn't control. The fact that the Christmas holidays had meant Adam was at home more had made Christmas a time to be dreaded for her and her children. It was a time of constant verbal abuse for her children and worse for her.

With just over two weeks to go she had started a Christmas list: ribbons and bows and the most gorgeous wrapping paper she could find were at the top before a small list of ideas for her children. With Matthew and John, she had splashed out. She had wanted to get them something special, something they could keep as a thank you for all they had done for her and her children. So, after a chat with

Maggie and some investigating, she had found a gentleman a few miles away who dabbled in oil painting in his spare time and took commissions. She had taken Maggie along to the initial visit for a second opinion as Kate had only heard about him by reputation. The two ladies had had quite a laugh as they drove up through the trees to the viewpoint Matthew had taken Kate to months before. After taking countless photographs on Kate's phone they had retreated down the mountain and onto the address Maggie had managed to get through a friend.

Once there, though, Kate needn't have worried. A tall, slim man in his fifties greeted them at the door and led them through to a small room at the back of his house. Functioning as a small gallery, the walls were lined with landscapes and portraits and Kate could see that his work would sit beautifully in the ranch house. So, after downloading the photos onto his laptop he and Kate discussed her commission: a landscape painting of the ranch from the viewpoint that had been so special to Matthew, his father and grandfather. She and Maggie were heading back to collect it this afternoon and she couldn't wait to see it.

For Kate, Christmas had begun the day after Thanksgiving. There was now a giant Christmas tree in the living room between the fireplace and the first of the windows and it caught her eye each time she left the office. She often wandered in just to look at it, just to enjoy it and soak up the peaceful atmosphere. Gold-coloured tinsel and assorted decorations in reds, greens and golds – some were old family heirlooms, others more modern – sparkled with the reflection from the fairy lights. The entrance hallway and banister were lined with garlands and wreaths that spilled through the rest of the ranch house, giving Kate and her children a Christmas they would never forget. Emma had also put a small tree on the island in the kitchen. Although according to Matthew that was a first, so Kate knew that had been done purely for her children's benefit. Emma's baking had also taken on a festive theme with cookies and pancakes being served in the shapes of Christmas trees, stars, stockings and snowmen.

A few hours later the usual Friday morning meeting was over, and Kate and Maggie were on their way back from collecting the oil painting. She knew she had spent more than she should have but John and Matthew had turned her and her children's world around, giving them a life they could only have dreamed of. For Kate, this gift was a one-off from her and her children for John, Matthew and future generations of Wester Lakes to enjoy.

As she dropped Maggie off, Kate popped in to say a quick hello to Walter before heading back to the ranch. She carefully hid the oil painting in the back of her closet and, after grabbing a cup of coffee, headed into the office. She still had an hour before she needed to meet Jake and Lucy from the school bus and she had a to-do list she was determined to get through.

Matthew, however, had other plans. "Ah good, you're back, have you got a minute? I've had an idea," he announced, rushing through the door.

"Yeah," she replied suspiciously, rising from her chair in time for him to wrap his arms around her waist. "What are you up to now, Mr Harrison?"

"Have you had any thoughts about Jake and Lucy's Christmas?"

"Sort of. I know Lucy would love anything crafty, so I thought about making up a box full of arts and crafts, pencils and stickers and glue and—"

"What about a bike each?"

"Oh no, that's far too much, they've never had anything that big at Christmas. Adam didn't bother so they won't be looking for anything like that. They can't ride anyway, they've never had one – that would have meant playing outside, and that was more than our lives were worth with Adam."

"I know, but every kid should have a bike and there is so much space here. They can't grow up never having had a bike!"

Kate knew that she could just afford two bikes if she was sensible, as she had been good and saved a little every month while still paying her way. But given her children had come to Colorado Springs with virtually nothing there were more practical things she could think of, not to mention the fact that she had just spent more than she normally would on Matthew and John – big expenses such as bikes weren't in her planned budget.

"What do you think, don't you think they would love one?"

She looked at his excited expression. His passion and love for her children was, to her, far more important than any bike.

She knew what it was like to live in another world, another reality, and she was so grateful for the little things that the bigger things never really entered her head. But perhaps Matthew was right. Why should her children go without such a wonderful surprise because of Adam and the way he had treated them? "Okay, let's do it," she gushed.

"Great, we could go into town first thing Monday once the kids are in school."

"Okay but…"

Matthew cut her off; he knew exactly what she was about to say. "Can we go half each, so they are from both of us, please?"

Nodding, she wrapped her arms around his neck and held him close. This year she felt she was getting all her Christmases in one. The memories of all her horrendous years in New York were slowly starting to fade, starting to feel as though they were in a surreal past that no longer belonged to her. She hoped that one day the effects of Adam's physical behaviour towards her would also start to fade.

20

Christmas morning had finally arrived at Wester Lakes. Blake and the younger ranch hands had gone home to their families for Christmas while Emma and Jesse stayed on at the ranch.

Jake woke up just as Matthew, John and Jesse were returning from the cattle sheds. Kate was just finishing getting dressed and could hear him running down the hallway into his sister's bedroom. Five minutes later, John, Matthew, Kate and her children were sitting round the Christmas tree opening presents.

Kate couldn't help but think about Adam as she watched her children opening their stockings before tucking into their presents. It was unlike any Christmas they had ever had. Jake, who was slightly overwhelmed at the whole event, tore at the wrapping paper, revealing an array of gifts. Some he desperately needed and others he had wished for but would never have asked for, and he couldn't quite believe that they all lay in front of him now. The highlight was a model tractor, a replica of the one Blake used out on the ranch.

Meanwhile Lucy was still unwrapping her gifts. She'd had a different approach – she was opening one and playing with it for a little while before going onto the next. The highlight for her though was a puppet set with a little wooden stage and an array of puppets and costumes to dress as she wished.

John, Matthew and Kate sat back and chatted with a mug of coffee in hand as they watched Jake and Lucy playing contentedly with their gifts.

"Right, your turn," Matthew said, reaching out to pick up a small box from under the tree. "Before you give me a row for buying something that's not practical, it's something special, something you would never buy yourself."

Kate slowly unwrapped the box. Tears sprang into her eyes as she looked down at the white gold and mother of pearl pendant and chain with matching bracelet. She remembered admiring the set weeks ago in town while she and Matthew waited to get a battery put into his watch. "How did you know?"

"You looked at it three times in the time we were in there – it's the only thing you went back to."

Kate closed her eyes as she held him close, absorbing the moment. She had no jewellery, only her wedding ring, which she hadn't worn since the day she left New York.

"I have something but it's for both of you. It's a thank you as well as a Christmas present from Jake, Lucy and me." Jake got up and helped his mum fetch the painting from behind the tree. She had wrapped it in bubble wrap before adding a layer of Christmas paper and a large bow.

Matthew sat beside his dad as they were handed their gift. There were a few moments of chatter about what on earth it could possibly be as they fought firstly with the wrapping paper and then with the bubble wrap. As the last of the bubble wrap fell away Matthew and John looked on, both speechless and both a little emotional. The oil painting had captured the colours of fall and the beauty of their ranch perfectly and both Matthew and John felt instantly transported to their much-loved viewpoint. They couldn't believe how much detail had been captured and were full of questions about the artist and how Kate had managed to find him. It was such an unexpected gift and was something that they both truly appreciated. Lots of thanks were shared as everyone hugged and chatted about the painting and their presents.

Finally, Kate rose from the sofa. "I presume no one has looked outside this morning?"

Jake and Lucy, who were still on the floor playing with their new gifts, looked up and shook their heads, eyes wide.

"Well, I think maybe you should," Kate suggested, nodding towards the window.

"Why?" Lucy gushed as she made her way across the floor, but her brother was already there.

The children gasped. "For us?" Lucy asked excitedly.

"Yup," replied Matthew. But he was watching Jake. He could tell he was both delighted and apprehensive at the same time. "It's okay, Jake, if you and Lucy want to go out on them now Dad and I will teach you how to ride."

"We'll have you riding in no time, I promise," John said, getting to his feet and clapping his hands together. "Go get your coats and boots on and we'll make a start."

"In our pyjamas?" Lucy asked cautiously.

"Of course in your pyjamas, it's Christmas!" John laughed.

Jake and Lucy ran out, fuelled with excitement, John following on behind. Kate laughed as she hugged Matthew. "Thank you for a wonderful morning, Mr Harrison."

A few hours later, Jake and Lucy were dressed and back out on their bikes with Matthew. Jesse and John were just returning from seeing to the cattle and horses and Emma and Kate were in the kitchen preparing the Christmas dinner. Kate was putting the finishing touches to the table when the doorbell rang.

"Oh, they're here!" Emma exclaimed as she dashed to the door.

Quite a few minutes later Emma returned. "Kate, I would like you to meet Todd, our oldest, and his wife Libby. And this is Charlie, our grandson," she said, giving Charlie a hug. Kate had already met their daughter Sarah and her husband Daniel, and it was lovely to see them again too.

Jesse and Emma's children were just a few years younger than Matthew and had grown up on the ranch, but they had both gone to university in Denver and had settled there. Todd had done quite well for himself and had been moved to Washington with his work on a two-year secondment, so this was the first visit home for him in a while and Emma was fit to burst at having all her family around her again.

As the afternoon passed, Christmas dinner was enjoyed by all. The table was filled with laughter and stories and although Kate and her children had only arrived at the ranch a few months earlier the feeling of family was strong amongst the group, some of whom had known each other for years, others having only just met. Jake and Lucy had a new friend in Charlie and Kate was enjoying Sarah and Libby's company. John sat at the head of the table, surrogate grandfather and uncle, and was obviously very close to everyone. For Kate, it wasn't about the gifts, it was about this moment, about everyone being together and happy, getting along and loving each other.

21

It was now the start of January and snow was falling heavily over Wester Lakes. The magnificent mountains that Kate loved so much were now covered in a layer of snow and had taken on a whole new beauty. As Kate looked up at them from the warmth of the truck she couldn't imagine living anywhere else.

Matthew ran out from one of the cattle sheds and jumped into the passenger seat. "Always looking at the mountains," he joked.

They chatted as Kate drove down towards the bunkhouses. The builders had been in for just under two weeks prior to Christmas and Kate and Matthew were happy with how things were progressing. They had managed to get a decent-sized squad and all three bunkhouses were being worked on at the same time. If all went to plan, the kitchens, bathrooms, baseboards and internal doors would be finished by late January and the redecoration could start.

Matthew followed Kate as she ran towards the shelter of the nearest bunkhouse. As they wandered round they could see everything was slowly coming together. Pipework had needed to be replaced in all three bunkhouses, as had some of the windows, which had held things up slightly, but the bathrooms were almost complete, and they would be ready for the tiler by the end of next week.

After a quick chat with the contractor Kate and Matthew jumped back into the truck. This time Matthew drove. He was dropping Kate off at the ranch house before heading into town; he had an important appointment to keep. As Matthew pulled up outside the ranch house Kate leaned across and hugged him. "Don't worry, you'll be brilliant."

"I hope so. I just want to live up to her expectations, that's all."

"You will, she adores you."

Thirty minutes later and Matthew was pulling up again, this time at the entrance to the school. He grabbed a couple of visual props from the trunk that Kate had helped him prepare, just to make things a bit more interesting, before heading up the steps. He pressed the buzzer and when the door was released, walked inside.

"Matthew!" A very happy Lucy rushed to greet him and grabbed his empty hand.

"Hi, Lucy. Were you waiting for me?"

Lucy nodded excitedly. "We all get to walk our mums or dads to the classroom when they come in to talk."

The five-year-old's response drew a raised eyebrow from behind reception, but Matthew's heart had now fully melted, and he wasn't going to let her down.

"Just let me sign in and then you can lead the way." Matthew spotted the visitors' book at reception and filled in his name, date and time while small pleasantries were passed with the confused lady behind reception. Matthew then took hold of Lucy's hand again. "Okay, lead the way."

Lucy chatted the entire way down the corridor, stopping only to open her classroom door.

"Come in, come in." Mrs Walker greeted Matthew with a vigorous handshake. "We cannot thank you enough for giving us some of your precious time this morning, Mr Harrison."

"It's my pleasure," Matthew replied, laying out his props in the order of his talk.

Thirty minutes later Matthew had told Lucy and her classmates all about the day-to-day running of the ranch, how they cared for the animals, about calving season and the forestry side. How they all had to work as a team and how everyone working on the ranch had an important role to play.

He had managed to hold the children's attention throughout and their enthusiasm was evident when he spent another thirty minutes answering their many questions.

"Well, children," Mrs Walker said, getting up from her chair. "What do we say to Mr Harrison for his very inspiring talk this morning?"

"Thank you!" This was followed by a round of applause that resounded throughout the classroom.

"Mr Harrison, thank you, that was fantastic. Would you mind if I called on you again in the future? The children thoroughly enjoyed that, and it might fit nicely around future topic work."

"Not at all. Any time."

"Lucy, would you lead the way back to reception please?"

Lucy rushed forward and grabbed Matthew's empty hand again. She chatted about his visit all the way back up the corridor. Matthew stopped to sign out and thanked the lady behind reception before turning back to Lucy. As he crouched down in front of her she threw her arms around his neck and hugged him tightly.

"I will be waiting for you when you get off the bus, okay?" Lucy pulled her head back and nodded happily. "You had better get back to class."

Lucy nodded again and kissed Matthew on the cheek before turning and walking back down the corridor. Matthew watched until she reached her classroom door. She turned and gave him a big smile to match her big wave before opening the door. Matthew could relax – he had lived up to her expectations.

Matthew arrived back at the ranch house just as everyone was tucking into lunch. He hurried in the veranda doors and kissed Kate before going to wash his hands.

"Well, how did it go?" she asked as he took his seat at the table. Matthew was so lost in the moment that he didn't care who was around to hear.

"She called me one of the mums and dads, gave me a big hug and kissed me on the cheek when I left." His eyes filled up, as did Kate's.

John sat at the other end of the table nodding to himself quite happily. As someone on the outside looking in, he could see that although slowly, everything was coming together nicely.

22

Adam sat pounding his fists against the leather steering wheel. Hitting it repeatedly until his knuckles bled. Oblivious to the pain he continued pounding through his rage, the blood now running down his hands and wrists onto his shirt sleeves. Sweat poured from his red-veined forehead, and his eyes still bulged from a mix of rage and anguish. The anguish at another failed search. The anguish at not finding his Kate.

The pounding began to subside as he looked back over his shoulder at the elderly lady with the mint-green cardigan. She was still sitting behind the counter of her small café, exactly where he had left her. Another lady, a much younger lady, had now arrived and was trying to console her. He watched as the younger lady rushed to lock the café door and turn the welcome sign to closed before running back behind the counter and picking up the phone. It was now time for him to leave.

Adam hadn't meant to hurt her. It had just happened. How was he supposed to stop himself when she kept saying so many horrible things to him, and after he had gone to so much trouble? He knew he had done everything right, leaving his apartment in such a hurry and getting to the airport so quickly. It wasn't his fault, he was only looking for what was rightfully his.

Adam turned the key in the ignition. Blood was running through his fingers and he was struggling to grip the steering wheel as he turned the car around and drove back in the same direction he had come.

He repeated their conversation over and over in his head. She was not his Kate Thomas, he had accepted that, but when she had suggested that his Kate was better off without him, well that had been more than he could bear. His rage had soared, his temper erupting. But no matter what that woman had gone through he was still far worse off than her. After all, her black eye would heal, but he was still without his Kate.

An hour later and Adam was pulling up outside a service station. He needed to get cleaned up, change his bloodstained shirt and clean the blood from the steering wheel before returning the rental car and catching his flight back to New York. Quickly, he stepped from the car and put on his overcoat. He fastened the buttons to hide his shirt, then, pulling his suitcase from the car, walked inside. His demeanour had changed once again to one of successful businessman.

A few hours later Adam was walking back into his New York apartment. He had a renewed sense of urgency as he repacked his suitcase, replacing his used shirt. The suitcase was once again ready to go at a moment's notice. As was the norm, he hung his overcoat in the closet and undressed to his boxers and undershirt before throwing his pants into the usual corner of his bedroom; his bloodstained shirt, however, was thrown in the trash. He looked at his watch as he switched on his laptop. It was still early, only six forty-five in the evening. There were still plenty of searches to be made tonight.

23

It was now early February and Kate was putting the final touches to the bunkhouses while she waited for Matthew. She had just hung the last of the artwork and was adding soft furnishings and little trinkets she had bought in town. As Kate went from one bunkhouse to the next she gave each one a final inspection. She was proud of what they had achieved. Although all three bunkhouses had identical layouts – open-plan kitchen and living area with French doors leading out to a private patio, large dining table, wood-burning stove, three double bedrooms and a bathroom – each had its own colour scheme.

The first was decorated throughout in warm reds and burnt oranges, the second in warm ambers and golds and the third in greens and creams. All three were warm and inviting and Kate was excited at the prospect of letting them out. As she fluffed the last of the cushions she could hear Matthew's voice outside and wandered out to meet him.

He had gone back to the ranch house to collect Jen Morton. She worked with a holiday letting agency and had come to take the final details of the bunkhouses. If all went to plan Kate and Matthew were hoping to have everything finalised and have the bunkhouses included in the letting agency's catalogue by mid March.

"Good morning, Kate." A lady in her mid-fifties stood before her. She was far too well dressed for the ranch in her navy trouser suit and stiletto heels, but she gave a professional and businesslike impression.

"Good morning, Jen, it's a pleasure to finally meet you after all our telephone conversations."

"Likewise. I have to say it's beautiful out here. I'm looking forward to seeing inside."

"Well, let's start in here." Kate pointed towards the first in the row. "Are you taking pictures today?"

"Yes."

"Great, but absolutely none of us, not even from a distance – just the bunkhouses."

"Are you sure? It looks much better if people are in them, makes the properties look busy and popular."

Matthew stepped forward. "Just the bunkhouses will be fine, thank you."

An hour later details and photos had been taken of all three bunkhouses along with the surrounding area and they were all heading back towards the ranch house. Matthew explained how the access was to be changed.

"Permission has just come through officially allowing us to reopen the old road. The men will start working on that in a couple of weeks and we have a carpenter making a new sign for the entrance as we speak. We also plan to fence off an area of the river, allowing guests access for fishing, and we will put picnic benches there and a paved area for BBQs. We won't be able to start the fencing for a few weeks though, as the ground is far too hard just now."

"Great, once that's done email me a couple of photos and I will get them included on our website. You should be able to rent out all year round here if you choose to. It's an ideal location for walkers, climbers and skiers. Everything else is in order. I will get the page layout done and forward you a copy to approve before it goes into the catalogue and onto our website. With what you have achieved here we could also do an initial double-page spread. There would be an additional charge, but it would provide you with a platform to launch this side of your business from."

"That might be a good idea," Kate agreed. "It would kickstart our advertising campaign."

"Okay, I'll get our design team onto that and email it across at the same time as the page layout. Now that I've been out I can give you an idea of what to charge. I'll email a guide over to you and highlight the range I feel you fall into. What you charge is up to you, but if you charge too much you will put people off. On the other hand your bunkhouses are in excellent condition and in a fantastic location. Hopefully we will get you some guests from late spring, early summer onwards."

After polite goodbyes Matthew and Kate watched Jen drive off before heading into the ranch house for one of their Friday meetings with John.

He was sitting waiting at the kitchen table with coffee and cake already in hand. Kate laughed as she grabbed a mug for her and Matthew.

Matthew and Kate filled John in on their meeting with Jen and asked for his thoughts on advertising and the double-page spread before covering their other queries. John agreed the double-page spread would be a good place to start with their advertising and they could recycle the images in their own advertising.

"Before we finish up, Kate, I've had another thought. Would you cast your eyes over the veterinary supplies? Everything we have in stock we need but would you have a look at our records? We record when stock comes in, when we use it and if we have had to dispose of it because it has gone out of date. Would you look to see if we are over-ordering? Some things are seasonal, others come in with short expiry dates, but that's all noted too. You'll be able to see how often each item is used."

"Of course. I'll make a start on Monday."

"Great. Right, Matthew, we'd better go. Jesse will be looking for us."

Matthew kissed Kate before following his dad out the door. Kate watched his tall, muscular physique. He was perfect.

24

It was the end of another working day and Adam was just arriving home. He was still as immaculately dressed as when he had left that morning. As always, he had his ritual to follow and it was carried out in an almost robotic manner. Firstly, he deleted his lunchtime call to Kate from the answering machine before heading towards the small table which sat in front of the sofa. His laptop was sitting open and ready to go. As he bent down to switch it on he reached into his coat pocket and pulled out his mobile phone, placing it neatly next to his laptop. While he waited for his laptop to boot up he took his coat off and hung it perfectly in his closet along with his tie. His pants and shirt were once again thrown across the room and made the already large pile of unlaundered clothes even larger. Still wearing only his dark boxers and white undershirt he returned to the sofa ready to begin his nightly routine.

'Kate Thomas' was once again typed into the search engine. It spat out the usual list which he could now recite with his eyes closed if he chose to. However, this time there was a new entry. An entry for holiday lets in Colorado Springs.

A flush of scarlet spread across his face as an intense rage once again stirred inside him. Within minutes veins began to pop from his neck and sweat was beading from his forehead. He clicked on the entry and read the article. He reread it over and over, repeating aloud, "The Harrison family, the Harrison family, the Harrison family."

Nothing made sense. Why had the entry appeared today? He googled the holiday letting agency. Nothing, only Harrison. He googled Harrison ranch, Colorado Springs – only Harrison again. It didn't matter what Adam typed into the search engine, the only surname that appeared was Harrison. There was no sign of the names Kate or Thomas anywhere.

Adam's obsessive nature meant he couldn't let this go. There had to be a connection. There had to be a link somewhere in the background that he couldn't see. This was a fresh new lead and there was no way that he wasn't going to follow it up thoroughly. He continued his search and found the double-page spread that Matthew and Kate had authorised. He scanned quickly, hoping the words 'Kate Thomas' would jump out. Suddenly, in a small footnote that followed the article, Adam read: 'M Harrison and K Thomas'.

He paced his apartment, stepping over discarded food cartons and rubbish. He may have lived an immaculately clean and polite lifestyle outside, but the apartment had not been cleaned since the day Kate had left. He continued to pace. The more he thought that Kate might be living there, without him, the more his rage soared.

He returned to his laptop and searched the Colorado time zone. It was two hours behind New York which meant the holiday letting office may still be open. He reached for his mobile, his personality changing once again as if by the flick of a switch. His demeanour was now calm and controlled.

Slowly he dialled the number of the letting agency. After a few short rings his call was answered.

"Good evening, I'm enquiring about a holiday let you have available in early summer. I just need you to confirm it's the one I'm thinking of."

"Okay, which one are you looking at, sir?"

"The one at Wester Lakes Ranch near Colorado Springs."

"Good choice, sir, they are stunning over there and an ideal location if you like walking or climbing."

"Yes, and I'm hoping I have the right place. Is it run by Kate Thomas?"

"Well it's the Harrison family out there, but yes, Kate is involved too."

"Thank you. I will be back in touch regarding dates. Goodbye."

Adam hung up. He stood for a second, rooted to the spot as his rage once again spiralled out of control. Then, running towards his bedroom, he threw anything that got in his way. He looked at the suitcase all ready to go. It had been checked the previous night as part of his obsessive ritual, but he needed to check it again. Once he was confident he had everything he needed he carried it through to the hallway and set it beside the door.

Returning to the bedroom he picked up the pants and shirt that he had earlier thrown into the corner and got dressed again. He took his tie and coat from the closet and once dressed had his usual final check of his appearance in the mirror.

Walking back towards the door he picked up his suitcase. As if it was part of the clothing his demeanour was once again that of a calm and successful family man. He left his apartment.

25

It was just after lunch on a beautiful Sunday afternoon as Kate ushered her children back towards the kitchen. “Quickly, Emma is waiting for you.”

“Hello, children. Are you ready to make cookies?”

“And decorate them?” Lucy asked excitedly.

“Of course.”

“Thanks, Emma, we should only be an hour at the most.”

“No problem, dear, take as long as you need.”

Kate kissed both her children goodbye before rushing towards the office to collect Matthew. “Ready?” she asked, tucking her head round the door. Matthew grabbed his jacket from the back of his chair and followed Kate out the door.

A neighbour, Claire Brunton, had been employed as housekeeper for the bunkhouses and Kate and Matthew were on their way to meet her for a chat. In her early fifties, Claire had recently moved back to Colorado Springs to be closer to her family after the death of her husband three years before. Kate had met her a couple of times, but John and Matthew had known her and her family all their lives. John had been at school with her older brothers and had known her husband well. She was just a couple of years younger than John and could remember him coming about her house when they were teenagers. It meant Matthew and John trusted her and were happy to leave her to oversee the preparation of the bunkhouses for guests.

Pleasantries were passed back and forth as Kate and Matthew greeted Claire. "Please come in," Kate gestured as she unlocked the door of the first bunkhouse.

They showed Claire around before discussing her duties and giving her a full set of keys. Kate found Claire easy to talk to and could tell she was enthusiastic about the position. Claire's demeanour suggested that she had standards and Kate was sure that the bunkhouses would be immaculate under her care.

"We will give you online access to the diary so that you can see the arrival and departure dates of guests. If there are any special requests, we will put notes in there so that you can also see them. If you have any questions at all, please phone us anytime." Kate handed Claire a piece of paper with their contact numbers.

"If you can get your bank details to us we will also get you onto payroll," Matthew added.

Forty-five minutes later the trio left the bunkhouse and Matthew and Kate were delighted that another task could be ticked off their list. They waved goodbye to Claire as she drove out of the newly opened old road. Cody and Dylan had already made a start blocking the track from the bunkhouses to the ranch and had assured Matthew it would be completed the following day.

Kate had stopped as she always did to look back at the mountains. Matthew walked up behind her and wrapped his arms around her waist.

"You okay?"

"Oh, I'm more than okay," she said, turning and wrapping her arms around his neck. "I'd better get back though, I said to Emma I would only be an hour."

"Okay, I'll drop you off at the house then I'll come back down to the cattle sheds and give Jesse a hand."

They walked hand in hand back to the truck. As Matthew opened her door she leaned towards him and kissed him. He pulled her closer; their kiss was long and passionate and neither wanted to let go.

They chatted about the bunkhouse side of the business as they headed back towards the ranch house. They had just over two months until they had their first bookings and they hoped there would be enough work to keep Claire on.

"What happened to Claire's husband?"

"Heart attack, why?"

"Just wondering. How old is she?"

"A couple of years younger than Dad, I think." Matthew

turned and looked at Kate suspiciously; he could tell she was up to something. "Why?"

"She would be perfect for your dad."

"She would, would she?"

"Yup, she would."

Kate looked up to the mountains as Matthew continued up the track towards the outbuildings. Their peaks were still covered in snow and to Kate they were magical. As Matthew turned the last corner he caught sight of a silver rental car pulling up outside the ranch house. "Someone must be lost," he commented, nodding towards the car.

Kate didn't pay much attention but as Matthew drove closer she caught the outline of a male through the windscreen.

A wave of numbness spread across her body like a tidal wave. Her breathing became laboured and she felt sick. It was as though someone had punched her in the stomach, emptying her body of any breath. No matter how hard she tried she couldn't speak.

Matthew pulled up in front of the ranch house and all Kate could do before he jumped out the truck was nudge him with her elbow. He turned and looked at her. The colour had drained from her face. She was rigid with fear.

"Is that him?"

Kate could only nod.

Matthew pulled his phone from his pocket. "Dad, he's outside the ranch house. Bring the envelope."

Kate hadn't heard a word Matthew had said. By now she had ringing in her ears, felt ice cold, was shaking and her hands were tingling. Fear had consumed every inch of her body in a way she hadn't felt since she had left New York.

"Stay here. Look at me, Kate – *stay in here.*" Even if she'd wanted to leave the truck she couldn't.

Matthew jumped out. By this time Adam had seen Kate and was walking towards her side of the truck. As Adam and Kate made eye contact she recognised the look in his eyes; she knew this would be too much for him.

Matthew ran around the front of the truck and blocked Adam's way. "Stay where you are. Do not come any closer." Matthew's voice was strong and assertive as he stiffened his stance in front of Adam.

"Get the fuck out of my way!" Adam shouted.

Matthew didn't flinch. "This is my land and you are trespassing. For the last time, do not come any closer."

"This might be your land but that's my property in that truck." Adam was gesturing towards Kate and trying to push Matthew out the way. He kept pushing at Matthew's chest, but he would not be moved. He kept his stance in front of Adam.

"Get over here, Kate!" Adam screamed. "Get out of that fucking truck and get in the car! Now!"

Matthew stepped forward, his broad shoulders making Adam look far smaller in comparison. He stepped forward again, giving Adam no option but to step back. Matthew wanted to get more distance between Adam and the truck.

"What the fuck are you doing? Get the fuck out of my way!" Adam screamed as he swung a fist at Matthew. The fact he missed only heightened Adam's rage. "I'm gonna fucking kill you! Get out of my way!"

John came running out of the ranch house and handed Matthew an envelope before moving towards the truck. He stood outside Kate's door as if to stand guard.

Kate was still unable to move. Palpitations were pounding inside her chest and she felt as though it was going to explode. Cody had heard Adam screaming and came running out from one of the outbuildings. He pulled out his phone and called Blake as he ran towards Matthew and stood at his side.

"Get out of the fucking way. She is mine and she is coming back with me."

"Kate decides what Kate does, no one else."

"Come here, Kate. Now. You want to be with me. You fucking love me. You fucking want me. Get over here. Get in the fucking car, now."

Minutes later the noise of tyres screeching to a halt brought Kate from her trance. She watched as Blake, Owen, Jesse, Dylan and Jason jumped from a truck and ran forward. They joined Cody and formed a line either side of Matthew as if forming a barrier between Adam and Kate. Adam was standing just three feet away from Matthew, his temper clear for all to see.

"I don't care how many of you there are, she is fucking coming with me. She's mine."

"Kate has made her decision – she has stayed in the truck," Matthew replied calmly but assertively. A stark contradiction to Adam, whose rage had now reached new heights.

But his rage was now also mixed with panic. "No. No. It's me she wants, me. She wants me."

"I know what you've done."

"You know fuck all! I've done nothing!" Adam screamed. "Kate, get out of the fucking truck now before I drag you out myself! Do you hear me? I will kick this arsehole out my way and I will drag you out myself!" Adam's voice was now hoarse, strained from shouting.

Matthew stood his ground. "I know what you've done to Kate and I have proof."

Adam fell silent. His eyes narrowed as he looked at Matthew. "You don't have proof, you're full of shit."

"I have proof and the only reason you are not behind bars is because I don't want to be the one who puts her children's father in jail. But if I have to I will."

"What the fuck are you talking about? There's no proof."

John watched from the truck as Adam's rage rocketed further still. The look in his eyes was of a man possessed, his stance now crooked, and he was drooling as he spoke. John realised that they were dealing with no ordinary jealous husband. Adam had more serious problems and they were going to have to ensure they got the better of him – today. Matthew had come to the same conclusion.

John pulled his phone from his jacket pocket and made a call. Kate watched as Matthew took a few steps closer to Adam, the ranch hands stepping forward with him. Matthew looked right into Adam's eyes and spoke sternly.

“I have proof and if I have to use it I will.”

“If you had proof you would have used it by now.”

Matthew knew he had to be convincing. He couldn’t blow this. “What, and put Kate through the courts? She fought hard enough to get away from you. Do you think I’d want to put her back in the same room as you again?”

“You’re bluffing, and what the fuck has it got to do with you anyway?”

“I have video evidence.”

Adam froze, his stance still crooked but now still, the expression on his face turning from temper to fear. “Wh-what?”

“Kate could sense it was going to happen again and she set a video camera. She mailed it to me the next day.”

John and Kate looked at each other; she shook her head almost imperceptibly as if to say no.

“Okay, well, we go with it,” John whispered. “Matthew obviously has something up his sleeve.”

Adam staggered on his feet. “What? No, no Kate doesn’t have a video camera.”

Matthew knew he had to keep the upper hand.

“No, but I do, and Kate and I go way back. Further back than you.”

These words only fuelled Adam’s temper further and his eyes appeared to glaze over as though he had been possessed from within.

Adam looked towards Kate one more time. Veins were bulging out from his forehead and neck. He had now lost all control. “Is this true? Kate? Is this fucking true? You are a fucking bitch! A fucking bitch!" he screamed at her, his fists gesturing towards her.

"Your face is there for everyone to see. Your voice too. We can hear every word." Matthew never dropped his gaze. His eyes were locked onto Adam's. He had held his stance throughout and his voice hadn't faltered.

Suddenly the front door of the ranch house opened. Jake walked out onto the veranda and looked at his dad. There was no emotion from either him or Adam. Kate leapt from the truck. "No, no, Jake, go back inside please. Please, go back inside!" she screamed through her sobs.

"The boy wants to come with me, don't you, boy? You know you want to come with me. Come here, boy, now."

Matthew was sure Adam didn't want Jake, but he knew Adam would be thinking Kate would go back with him if her son did.

Jake looked down as he slowly walked down the steps of the veranda. Matthew nodded to Blake, who was at the end of the barrier nearest to Jake. He would grab Jake before he reached Adam if he had to. Kate screamed, "No!" and went to run to Jake, but John grabbed her.

"No, Kate." John held her tight. "Leave it to Matthew. Trust him."

"Come on, boy, quicker!" Adam screamed.

Kate watched as Jake reached the bottom step. He didn't look at his dad. Instead he raised his head and looked at Matthew, straight into his eyes, and Matthew kept his gaze. Jake walked forward slowly and, instead of walking towards

Adam, he went to Matthew. He squeezed himself in between Matthew and Cody and slid his hand into Matthew's. Matthew held it tight and returned his gaze to Adam.

"Jake has made his decision. He is staying here."

John could feel Kate's body sink with relief as she fell to the ground. She had almost lost consciousness. John shook her gently, trying to keep her roused.

"For fuck's sake, Kate, get up! Get in the fucking car. You are making a scene!" Adam screamed again. "You are making a fucking scene!"

"There is enough evidence to put you behind bars for ten to fifteen years. We haven't used it yet but if we have to we will." Matthew's voice was still strong, firm and authoritative.

"Who the fuck do you think you are, her keeper?"

"No, I'm her lawyer and I'm a damn good one. In this envelope are copies of papers that have already been submitted to the courts requesting a restraining order be put in place prohibiting you from coming within two hundred meters of the boundaries of this ranch. There is also a copy of another document. I couldn't submit it until you came near Kate but now you have, it will be submitted first thing tomorrow morning. It's requesting another restraining order preventing you from approaching Kate or the children. You come near any of us again and the video evidence will be used. I give you my word on that."

Kate struggled to her feet.

"What are you doing?" John asked, helping her up.

"I can't let him leave thinking he has done this to me

again. I need to show him I'm stronger. That I am where I want to be. That he doesn't have power over me anymore."

Kate put one foot in front of the other. Her legs were numb. She couldn't feel the ground below her feet. John stayed with her, kept her pace. As she approached the barrier she nudged herself in between Matthew and Owen. She clutched hold of Matthew's arm. Both Matthew and Owen could feel her body shaking. Matthew kept his gaze on Adam and was aware of Owen putting a supporting arm around Kate. John took his place at the end of the line.

"One last thing." Matthew put Jake's hand in Kate's and stepped closer to Adam. He took a document out of the envelope. "This one you sign, right here, right now, and I keep it."

"What the fuck is that? I'm not signing anything."

"Kate is serving you with divorce papers. You will sign it now. I have another copy if we need it so don't bother trying to be clever. You won't leave here until I have a signed copy, so you may as well get it over with now."

Adam looked at Kate. She looked straight into Adam's eyes and stepped forward so she was level with Matthew and took his hand as if to reinforce to Adam where she belonged and who with.

Everyone was distracted by the sound of another car coming down the driveway. It was a police car. An officer in his mid-fifties stepped out, accompanied by a younger officer who had been driving. The older officer was obviously in charge. He walked across to Adam and slowly looked him up and down.

"Sir, I believe you have been asked to leave this property and you have refused. I also believe you are insisting this lady comes with you against her will. I suggest you leave this property now willingly or you will be arrested for trespassing."

"She's my wife!" Adam screamed at the officer.

Matthew turned to face the officer. "Mrs Thomas is filing for divorce, we have the papers here. We had hoped that under the circumstances Mr Thomas would sign them before he left."

The officer turned to Kate. He could see the fear in her eyes. "Is this true?"

"Yes, yes. My children and I escaped him once. We are not going back." She turned to Adam, her voice trembling. "Let me go. Sign the papers, please."

Adam's temper hit an all-time high as he lunged towards Kate with both fists raised. Matthew pulled Kate out of his way as the two officers ran forward and grabbed Adam. They pulled him back and the younger officer restrained him while the older officer grabbed his cuffs. He didn't cuff Adam, instead he held them to reinforce to Adam the trouble he was getting himself into.

The senior officer's demeanour changed as he met Adam's gaze. "Now, sir, now it's getting serious. That's both trespassing and attempted assault."

Matthew walked across to the older policeman. "We will press no charges if Mr Thomas signs the divorce papers now and leaves quietly."

The officer turned to Adam; he couldn't get involved in the signing of the paperwork. Adam had the right to make his own decision there, but he could see Adam knew he had been beaten as he nodded towards the document in Matthew's hand. Matthew laid the paperwork out on the hood of Adam's rental car. The younger officer released his grip and Adam walked towards the car, but instead of signing the paperwork his temper fuelled and he lashed out, forcing the papers to scatter across the hood onto the ground.

Matthew looked at Adam and laughed. "That's fine, that's absolutely fine," he said, calmly picking up the paperwork and placing it back on the hood. "If this is how you want to do things then we'll see you in court. I'm sure you won't be in there long given the video evidence."

At that, Adam's gaze fell to the papers. He knew it was over; he had lost. Slowly he reached for the pen and signed where Matthew indicated.

Matthew returned to the barrier and took his place between Kate and Jake, taking hold of their hands as the older policeman spoke to Adam. They watched as Adam got into his car and drove off without looking back.

The senior policeman turned to Kate. "Are you alright, miss?"

"I am now, thank you."

"Okay. Well we'll go and catch up with Mr Thomas, make sure he heads back to the airport and keeps himself out of trouble."

The barrier was held until both cars were out of sight. Everyone was silent as if trying to digest what had just happened. John was first to speak.

"Right, men, let's go inside. I'm sure you will agree we could all do with a stiff drink. Matthew, Kate, Jake, we will see you when you're ready." He ushered the men towards the side of the house.

Kate was down on her knees hugging Jake. Matthew dropped beside them and pulled them in close. There was stunned silence as relief began to leave their bodies. Matthew held on to them as tight as he could, as if never wanting to let either of them go. He could feel Kate shaking uncontrollably. Jake was the first to speak.

"Are you okay, Mum?"

"You're asking if I'm okay? Are you okay?"

"We were always going to be okay, Mum. Matthew was always going to sort him out," Jake replied in a much calmer tone than Kate had expected.

Matthew looked at Jake. He had tears in his eyes. "I am very proud of you, Jake. What you did today took courage. I love you, Jake, always remember that."

Jake threw his arms around Matthew's neck and Matthew lifted him up with one arm and pulled Kate up with the other. "Come on, let's get you both inside."

Kate couldn't speak. She was sobbing again as she watched Matthew and Jake together. But this time her sobs were different. She felt as though a weight had been lifted and she realised she'd been carrying an unacknowledged guilt. Despite knowing she had made the best choice for herself and her children, the guilt of taking her children from their father had finally been lifted. Today Jake had spoken for himself with his own actions and she now knew this was the family he wanted too.

Matthew walked them slowly up the steps and into the ranch house. He led them towards the kitchen but stopped short of the door. He looked at Kate. She tightened her grip on his arm. "It's okay, I want to go in."

Silence fell across the room as they entered. Emma was finishing putting snacks on the table and Lucy was still sitting where Kate had left her a couple of hours before. She was none the wiser to the afternoon's events. Matthew put Jake down and he rushed towards his sister, grabbing one of the cookies they had made as he sat down beside her.

Emma pushed a mug of hot sweet tea into Kate's hands and told her to drink it quickly as Matthew led Kate round to the two empty chairs. He stood and looked at the men around the table as Kate took a seat. They could only sit in quiet disbelief at the scene they had just witnessed.

"I can't thank you all enough for what you did out there," he said. "You all went above and beyond. I'm not thanking you as your employer, I'm thanking you as your friend. What you did, it means a lot." Matthew left it at that; he didn't want to say any more while Kate and the children were around but he knew he would catch up with the men later.

The men murmured awkwardly that it was no problem, but the truth was they didn't know what to say. They had all had an insight into Kate's past and could hazard a guess at what she and her children had been through. They were all relieved they had been there to help, and each one of them would do it again.

Kate was also aware of the insight they'd had and for the first time that didn't matter. Now the shame she had felt for years was no longer her shame, it was Adam's. She finally felt free. She was still shaking and watching Jake like a hawk, but at the same time she had an immense feeling of relief.

John stood up, and looking at Emma he gave a small nod towards the children and then to the door leading through to the hallway. Emma quickly asked the children to follow her and Kate watched as Jake followed Emma out the door giggling with his sister.

"Right, men, off you go, take the rest of the afternoon off. You've more than earned it."

His men had other ideas. They stood up and Blake looked at his watch. "Is that the time? We'd better get back to work, lads. Lots to do."

John patted each of them on their back and shook their hand as they walked out through the veranda doors and back to work. Closing the doors behind them John took a seat opposite Kate and Matthew.

Kate was leaning against Matthew with her head on his shoulder. His arm was around her, still holding her close.

There was silence for a few moments before Kate lifted her head slightly and spoke for the first time since they had come in.

"I don't understand what happened out there. What video? There's no video."

Matthew looked at her. "Adam doesn't know that," he replied softly.

Kate returned his gaze. She was beginning to make sense of what had just happened.

"Kate, he is a dangerous man in a dangerous state of mind. We couldn't let him leave here today thinking he could come back." He added softly, "We had no option but to win that fight today."

"And the police?" Kate asked, confused.

"The older one is a very good friend of mine – we were at school together. I just gave him a quick call," John said as he stood up and headed towards the veranda doors. "Right, I'm going to leave you two alone. What if I take Jake and Lucy out with me? I could tell them I have to check the forest, they like a drive up there. I will keep an extra eye on Jake, I promise. We won't be back until dinner's ready."

"Okay, but let me see them before you go?" Kate smiled gratefully.

26

Kate was still leaning against Matthew when Emma returned to clear the table. "Would you like another tea, dear? You're still shaking."

Matthew could feel her. The shaking hadn't subsided, and she was still ash white. "Maybe a small Scotch, Emma, she might be in shock."

Emma quickly went to fetch a bottle, poured a little into a glass and put it into Kate's hands. She drank it quickly without saying a word.

"Come on, you're going to lie down for a while," Matthew instructed, helping Kate to her feet.

Kate felt faint, as though an uncontrollable unconsciousness had taken over her body. Relief was setting in. Years of abuse was now at an end and Matthew had instigated her divorce. She could, for the first time in years, let her guard down. Stop talking with caution and stop covering up her past. She was finally safe. She was finally free.

Matthew opened her bedroom door and guided her inside. She was still covered in muck from the road outside, so he helped her undress to her underwear and pulled back the duvet. She fell onto her bed as though she was a rag and Matthew pulled the duvet back over her. He sat on the edge beside her and pulled her hair away from her face, and within minutes she was asleep.

Matthew returned to the kitchen to speak to Emma. She had heard everything but had managed to convince Lucy it was just the television in another room.

"I think she's gone into shock so I'm going to stay with her. I'll take some work from the office and I'll be on her sofa if anyone's looking for me."

"Okay, dear, I'll bring you a coffee in a while."

Matthew settled on Kate's sofa. He opened mail and read brochures that he had been ignoring for long enough and started putting an order together for feed. Kate was still sound asleep when Jake and Lucy came back for dinner. They came in to see her but even their chatter didn't cause her to stir. Matthew listened as they sat either side of him, telling him about their *adventure* through the forest. A few minutes later there was a knock on the door.

John popped his head round. "Anyone coming for dinner?"

Jake and Lucy jumped up and headed out the door.

"Wash your hands first," Matthew whispered as he followed them out into the hallway. Once they'd run ahead he turned to his father. "How was Jake?"

"Inconceivably, he was fine. I asked him if he was upset about what had happened and he just said his dad always shouts. I think what we saw today, son, was normal behaviour."

Matthew agreed. "Okay, well I'm going to stay here. I don't want Kate waking up alone."

"Fine, son, I'll get Emma to bring you some dinner and I'll take Jake and Lucy back out with me to check the cattle once dinner is done."

As Matthew settled back down on the sofa Emma appeared with a tray and left him his dinner and another mug of coffee. A good while later, Matthew was nodding off when Jake and Lucy returned from checking the cattle.

Matthew listened to their stories and helped them get showered and ready for their beds. He brushed Lucy's hair and helped her blow-dry it before taking them both up to the kitchen for supper.

"Hi, son, Kate still asleep?"

"Absolutely sound. A bomb could go off and I reckon she'd sleep through it."

"Special treat tonight," Emma said, putting a plate of freshly made chocolate-chip pancakes down on the table between Jake and Lucy.

Matthew watched as they both took a pancake. He looked at Lucy, who was always so bubbly and never without a smile. He wondered if she had been this happy in New York. After what Matthew had witnessed today he found that unimaginable.

"Is Mum alright?" Jake asked, turning to look at Matthew as he took a second pancake.

"Yes, she's just tired. She needed a lie-down, that's all."

"It's so different here."

Silence fell across the table. The ranch hands were unsure what to do or say. John watched as Matthew put a reassuring hand on Jake's shoulder.

"Well, we do things differently around here, Jake, that's all. We treat people the way we would like to be treated ourselves and we look after one another."

Jake looked at Matthew, his eyes and smile enough for Matthew to know he understood.

"You will always be safe here, you know that, don't you?" Jake nodded and finished his pancake.

"Right, you two, say goodnight, it's time for bed."

Goodnights said, Matthew walked them back out into the hallway.

He looked in on Kate, who was still sound asleep, before following Lucy into her bedroom. Lucy gave him her usual big smile and a tight hug before grabbing her teddy and jumping into bed.

"Do you know who that teddy belonged to before he was yours?"

Lucy shook her head, cuddling her teddy tighter.

"He was my mum's. He used to sit on a chair in her bedroom when I was little. I think she would be very happy that you love him as much as you do." Matthew kissed her on the forehead. "Goodnight, Lucy."

Matthew went to check on Jake. He had already got himself into bed, but he was sitting up as if he wanted to talk.

"You okay?" Matthew asked as he sat down on the edge of the bed beside Jake. Jake nodded. "You sure? It's been an unusual day."

"I had forgotten what it was like when Dad was with us. He always shouts, about everything."

"Yeah, I found that out today."

"He was always worse with Mum though."

Matthew wasn't sure how to respond. "Well, you are all here now and you are safe."

"How long have you known Mum?"

"About thirteen years. We were at university together in New York."

"Is this what other families are like?"

Matthew looked at Jake, who suddenly looked so small and vulnerable. "Yes Jake. I know I'm not your real dad, but I love you and I care about you as if you were my own."

Jake leaned forward and gave Matthew a hug. Matthew hugged him back until Jake was ready to let go before pulling his duvet up like Kate did every night.

"I'm going to keep an eye on your mum, make sure she's okay when she wakes up. If you need me I'll be on her sofa."

Jake nodded.

Matthew grabbed a blanket from the bathroom closet before heading back to Kate's room. She was still sound asleep.

Her reaction had made him realise just how horrendous living with Adam must have been. For the relief of getting someone out of your life to have this effect then that life was unimaginable to Matthew.

Lying down on Kate's sofa he threw the blanket over himself and tried to focus on his book. Eventually he dozed off in the early hours before waking again to the sound of Kate stirring. She sat up, confused.

"Hey, it's okay," he said, leaping from the sofa to sit on the edge of the bed beside her.

"What time is it?"

"Just after four."

"Oh god, Jake and Lucy, where are they?"

"In bed, sound asleep."

The last Kate had known it was mid-afternoon – she had been asleep for thirteen hours. She leaned into him, nestling her head on his shoulder.

"You're cold."

"I've been on your sofa."

"I need to go stick my head round the kids' doors. I just need to see them." Kate got up, grabbed her robe and quickly ran out. Returning a few minutes later she jumped back into bed. "Come in here with me, it'll heat you up."

Still in his jeans and shirt Matthew got under the duvet. He wasn't risking Jake or Lucy walking in.

"How are you feeling?"

"I feel fine. I can't believe I slept for so long."

"You were in shock. Emma thinks it was also relief at

getting Adam out of your lives. She heard everything too you know."

"Oh no, what about Lucy?"

"Emma convinced her it was the television, she's absolutely fine."

"And Jake?"

"He's fine too. I asked him when I put him to bed but he spoke more about how different life is now without his dad."

"I knew he wouldn't be fazed by Adam – he's used to that. I'm worried because he saw him being followed off the ranch by the police."

"He never mentioned that."

"I might just let them lie in. Keep them off school just so I can keep an eye on Jake."

"He asked how you were at supper, said that life was different here. He was happy enough though. Emma made them chocolate-chip pancakes."

"I feel bad that I wasn't around when they came back. It was the weirdest feeling. It was as though my body shut down."

"Yeah, we gave you a Scotch and I brought you to lie down. You were asleep in minutes."

"I don't remember that. I hate Scotch."

"I helped Lucy dry her hair – that was a new experience for me." Matthew laughed. "Does that girl ever stop smiling?"

"You dried her hair?"

"Yeah."

"Mr Harrison, you are just too much."

"Excuse me, they were both showered and fed and absolutely fine, thank you very much," he joked defensively.

Kate cuddled into him and they both dozed until her alarm sprang to life at six o'clock. Kate got up and went for her shower while Matthew ran upstairs for his.

Thirty minutes later Kate had dried her hair and was putting on some make-up. Today was a brand-new day. The start of a brand-new life where she could be Kate Thomas if she needed to be. She could say her name out loud, sign for a delivery legibly, rather than the usual scribble that no one could decipher. Today she could just be.

As soon as she was ready she checked on Jake and Lucy. They were still sound asleep, Lucy still cuddling her teddy. Kate ran upstairs two at a time and headed into Matthew's room. He had just finished getting ready and was delighted to see Kate looking so relaxed and happy. He, on the other hand, was exhausted after his few hours' sleep. "Coffee?" he enquired.

Kate nodded. "Absolutely."

They were first in the kitchen. "It's not often we beat Emma," Matthew exclaimed as he and Kate got the coffee going. They were sitting at the table, coffee in hand, when everyone else started to appear. Emma was first. She walked straight over to Kate and gave her a hug. She didn't say anything, she didn't have to, and Kate got up and helped her start breakfast.

John was next. "Morning, Kate. Did you sleep okay?"

"Sleep?" Matthew quipped jokily. "She was virtually unconscious for thirteen hours."

Once the table had filled, Kate walked round and stood beside her chair.

"While the children aren't here I just wanted to thank you all for yesterday. You were all there for me and Jake and I can't begin to put into words how much that means to us. Jake is far more aware than you realise, and I know it will have meant a lot to him too. We were always very much alone in New York with Adam, but yesterday, well, I will never be able to thank you enough for what you did. All of you."

"How is Jake this morning?" John enquired. "He was absolutely fine last night, and I wasn't sure if that was a good thing or a bad thing."

"I've left them both to sleep this morning, they aren't going to school. I wanted to keep an eye on Jake. Adam's behaviour won't have fazed him in the least, I know that. He is more than used to Adam's temper." Everyone looked at each other, all thinking the same. All aware of the horror of Kate and her children's previous life. "But I don't know how he feels about seeing his dad followed off the ranch by the police. Although I'm hoping it might have helped finalise things for him too."

"Well, Kate, I know I've said it before but here is to our table and to all who sit around it. I wouldn't have it any other way." John raised his coffee mug.

The sound of bare feet running into the kitchen turned everyone's heads. Lucy, still wearing her pyjamas and hugging her teddy with one arm, ran to her mum with her usual beaming smile. Kate, who was still standing, crouched down and gave her daughter a hug. Lucy kissed her mum before running around to Matthew. Everyone watched as she climbed onto his knee and snuggled in. She sat there, still half asleep, while Matthew ate his breakfast one-handed. Occasionally she would pinch a bite of his breakfast as his hand brought his food past her mouth.

Kate watched. It was one of the most beautiful views she had ever seen. Even better than her precious views of the mountains.

27

Kate and her children spent the day together out on the ranch. They may have had the day off school but Kate had no intention of letting her children lie around.

They spent their morning helping Owen muck out the stables before Matthew helped them groom Annabel and Jasper. Much to Lucy's delight Matthew brought her a set of short steps to help her reach Annabel's mane and tail.

After lunch Matthew took them round to a clearing behind the outbuildings and bunkhouses. The clearing sat between the forest and the buildings and ran the entire length of the ranch.

"This is an area we keep clear in case there is a wildfire. We never keep vehicles or store anything round here. Hopefully, if there was a fire it would prevent it from spreading and protect all the buildings. When we get a chance, we spend a few hours clearing it of any weeds or grasses that have come up. We want it to be a clear dirt track, so nothing will burn. We have between now and the start of summer to clear anything that has come through since last autumn but it's too much to do at once, so we do it section by section when we can fit it in and then it's just keeping it clear of any spring growth."

Kate watched as her children got stuck in. She helped Lucy clear weeds away from the edges while Jake was in amongst the ranch hands. They had formed a line and were working together as they made their way up the track. This was something they had obviously done many times before and had a good system going. Owen was following along behind, raking and gathering up what the men had left. Every now and then someone would swap places with the person doing the gathering.

As the afternoon passed Jake did his best to keep up with the men, even doing a little raking and gathering himself. His enthusiasm more than made up for his lack in strength. The ranch hands spoke to him as though he was one of them and included him in their chat. Kate could see that the events of yesterday had, if anything, solidified his feelings of being at home at Wester Lakes. She could also see a change in the ranch hands, in the way they were interacting with both Jake and Lucy. It was as though yesterday's events had made them more protective towards them, as though her children had been absorbed fully in the extended ranch family.

As late afternoon approached the men had other jobs

they needed to see to before dinner and John offered to take Jake and Lucy down to the cattle sheds, giving Matthew and Kate some alone time. They walked down past the ranch house and onto the track with no ears. They walked slowly, arm in arm, chatting about the mountains, the children and the previous afternoon's events.

"Jake is amazing, he just keeps going," Matthew remarked. "He loves being part of whatever the men are doing."

"I know, I'm proud of him. Even after yesterday he just keeps trooping on."

"He is made of strong stuff."

"I know. We had to make our unit of three strong. Almost as if Adam was on the sidelines. I was lucky that because he was at work all day I could mould us, then we just had to put up with him in the evenings. Weekends were hard though. They were always very long days. I always hated a Friday. The whole weekend was still right in front of us on a Friday."

"I can't begin to imagine what it must have been like living with him. I can't believe that a child can become so used to a temper like that."

"As far as Adam is concerned that is all Jake has ever known. Lucy too."

"What about you? How are you feeling today?"

"I feel free." Kate turned to Matthew, her smile so broad it almost resembled Lucy's. "How come you had all the paperwork ready?"

"I had the restraining orders prepared months ago just in case, then when you said you would love a divorce I thought that if he did ever turn up here he would already know where you were. I thought we may as well be as prepared as possible. To be honest the holiday lets have worried me, a lot. I knew that as soon as we started letting them out we could have people from all over the country. I have to admit though, I didn't expect him to turn up before they were let."

"I can't thank you enough. To be rid of him is one thing but a divorce, I just can't believe it."

"Well, it's been a strange day today but tomorrow morning when the kids are in school we can get it all sorted out. You will have to sign the papers too though, is that okay?"

Kate stopped and wrapped her arms around Matthew. She trusted him completely, she always had, but what he had done for her, how he had stood up to Adam even before the ranch hands arrived, how he had managed the situation when Jake had walked out the house – it had all taken her trust in him to a whole new level. He had been as solid as a rock since the minute they had been reunited in the diner all those months before and he had just secured her freedom. Suddenly the feeling of being free seemed to reinforce her love for him. It was as though she was finally able to truly love him back, the way he did her, with nothing and no one standing in her way.

"Why are you looking at me like that?"

"I love you, Mr Harrison."

"I know, and I love you too," he replied, taking her face in his hands and kissing her tenderly. The surroundings faded into the background as they were consumed with a new hunger and passion, losing themselves in the moment.

Suddenly remembering where they were, they wandered back to the ranch house for dinner.

They arrived back at the same time as everyone else. After another full table and another family dinner Kate took Jake and Lucy for their showers while the men went back out to work. Once again, they were full of chatter about their day and Kate knew it had done Jake the world of good. While they showered she checked their bags were ready for school the next day and laid out their clothes.

Before long Lucy was sitting at the kitchen table colouring in and Jake was reading a book. Emma appeared in the kitchen to sort out some laundry and Kate took the chance to grab a quick shower herself before supper. She reappeared half an hour later, showered, dressed, hair blow-dried and wearing a little make-up.

Soon the table had filled again for supper and the chatter excited Lucy. Calving season was about to get underway with a few cows already showing the first signs of labour. For Lucy the wait was unbearable.

"We'll be out at all hours, checking the mothers and the calves. It will go on for weeks," John explained.

By this time Lucy had wandered round to John and climbed onto his knee. He was answering her many questions while Jake was asking Matthew if he would be able to help.

"Absolutely, as long as your homework's done first," Matthew replied happily, loving Jake's enthusiasm.

"Right, come on, you two, bedtime," Kate instructed, rising from the table.

This time Matthew got up and went with them. He followed Jake into his room while Kate followed Lucy into hers. Once goodnights were said Matthew and Kate passed each other in the hallway as they swapped rooms.

Goodnights said again, they met in the hallway and walked arm in arm back to the kitchen. Both Matthew and Kate knew that her little unit of three was now very much a solid unit of four.

Once supper was over the ranch hands dispersed and John wandered into the living room to catch up on television recordings and to read his book.

"Are you coming upstairs tonight?" Matthew asked.

"Yes, but I'll meet you up there. I just need to grab a couple of things first and I want to try phoning Alice. Hopefully the number I have for her is still correct. If not I'll phone the boutique tomorrow, but I'd much rather chat to her when she's at home and she can speak freely. I can't wait to tell her that we are all okay and happy. It will be so nice to be able to speak to her again, to chat like we used to."

"Okay, I'll nip into the office for ten minutes then I'll have a shower. See you when you're ready."

Forty minutes later Kate wandered into Matthew's room wearing her robe and carrying a large bag. He had just stepped out of the shower and had a towel wrapped around his waist.

"What on earth have you got in there?"

"Everything I need to get ready in the morning," she replied, walking up to him slowly and wrapping her arms around his neck. She had a different look in her eyes. It was a look Matthew couldn't quite decipher but was finding utterly irresistible.

She stepped back from him, untying her robe. It fell slowly from her shoulders, revealing her tall, lithe body. Matthew looked down at her flushed breasts and slender hips, an involuntary gasp escaping his lips.

She tugged at his towel until it fell to the floor. His strong masculine body was calling her, drawing her in and causing a yearning in her that she had not felt in years. Not since she had last been with Matthew. She stepped closer, feeling the warmth of his body on hers and his breath on her neck as he drew his lips up towards hers. He could smell her perfume, taste it on his lips as they caressed her skin.

She took him by the hand and led him towards the bed. He kept his body close to hers, mirroring her movements as she fell backwards. His strong shoulders that she had admired for so long were now all-encompassing as his muscled body rested between her thighs.

"Make love to me."

"Are you sure?" Matthew whispered, his lips kissing hers.

"Make love to me."

Matthew's lips travelled down Kate's body with an almost uncontrollable passion. Their need for each other was all-consuming as he entered her pleading body. Her back arched uncontrollably as she trembled, aching for him. She moaned as she ground herself into him, their warm sensual bodies loving each other into the small hours of the morning.

For Matthew it had finally given him the intimacy he

had yearned for with Kate. It had allowed him to give himself to her fully. To love her. To have her give herself back without hesitation, without fear. Their passions took them to heights neither had been to before. Their love for each other solidified as their bodies became one.

Matthew woke early the next morning. Kate had wrapped herself around him, her head resting on his chest. It was five-fifteen. They had forty-five minutes before they had to get up.

Caressing her arm until she roused Matthew did what he had wanted to do every morning since Kate had first come to lie with him. He rolled her onto her back and made love to her again. She wrapped her legs around him as if never letting him go. Their passion, if it was possible, was more intense than in the hours before as they became familiar and lost in each other once again.

28

Kate could barely contain her excitement as she stood at the arrivals gate of Colorado Springs Airport. It had now been almost six years since she had last seen Alice, but they had been chatting on the phone regularly in the few weeks since Kate had got back in touch and they felt as though they had never been apart.

Kate watched as parents and grandparents reunited with children and grandchildren. The contrast of lovers embracing and work colleagues shaking hands brought home to Kate the different worlds that came together to walk through the doors of the bustling airport. Travellers streamed through the arrivals gate at regular intervals and Kate watched on intently until she finally spotted Alice's short blonde bob amongst the crowd.

Alice hadn't changed a bit, a little older but still the same business-like city girl Kate remembered. The chatter didn't stop as they put Alice's luggage in the back of the truck and headed towards the highway and home to Wester Lakes.

Kate told Alice more about Matthew and her life since coming to Colorado Springs and Alice brought Kate up to date, detailing her now permanent breakup from on-off boyfriend Joe. The conversation switched quickly from one topic to another as they tried to catch up six years in a short space of time.

The chatter continued as Kate turned into Wester Lakes. Alice was in awe at the beauty and vastness of the ranch, but as the true city girl she was, she questioned how Kate coped with having so few people around. Kate chuckled and reminded her she saw far more people here than she ever did in New York. Kate carried on past the ranch house and round towards the cattle sheds. She stopped briefly to introduce Alice to Matthew but didn't linger as calving season was now in full swing and it was all hands on deck, before carrying on towards the renovated bunkhouses.

Alice had agreed to be a trial guest. Although she was coming to see Kate and her children it made sense to have her stay in one of the bunkhouses where she could soak up the atmosphere of visiting the ranch in return for an honest review. It would also give Alice more privacy and a chance to completely relax, although she was under strict instructions to come up to the ranch house for her meals and the two friends hoped to spend as much time together as possible during her visit.

"So, what do you think?" Kate asked, as she unlocked the door to the first of the three bunkhouses. Kate had chosen her personal favourite for Alice, the bunkhouse decorated in warm reds and burnt oranges.

"Oh, Kate, it's lovely," Alice insisted as she wandered from room to room. There was a multi-picture frame hanging in the hallway showing the bunkhouse through its various stages of renovation. The entire process was photographed in black and white with the final made-over images shown in colour. "Wow, what a transformation, Kate, it's gorgeous."

"There's also a welcome bottle of wine in the fridge," Kate winked. "Now, I know I should leave you to settle in first, but please come up to the house with me now. I can't wait for you to meet everyone and see Jake and Lucy."

Neither child knew Alice, but their mother had spoken to them often about 'Aunt Alice', so their family was about to get a little bigger once again.

"Come on then, I can't wait to see them either. I'll just grab my bag, I have a little something for them."

It wasn't long before Alice was sitting at the dining table enjoying Emma's delicious cooking. Jake and Lucy were happily chatting and joking with Alice, but it wasn't the dining experience they were all used to. Meal times were split during calving season as the cattle had to be watched twenty-four seven. Matthew, Jesse and Cody were first up but they were heading straight back out as soon as they were done to let the others up.

Matthew was enjoying listening to Kate and Alice

reminiscing about their early years in the boutique and he watched Kate with a mixture of pride and delight as happier memories from her past came flooding back. Soon though it was time for him to head back out and, after all her friend had been through, Alice couldn't hide her delight as he and Kate kissed each other goodbye before he turned to give Lucy a hug.

As Matthew was taking over cattle shed duty, where they kept the expectant mothers who needed extra looking after, Jake was allowed to go with him for a little while, to watch and learn and maybe help a bit when it was safe to do so. This, however, hadn't impressed Lucy, and Kate promised to take her down once she had helped Emma clear up after dinner.

The veranda doors soon swung open again as Blake and John appeared for their dinner. Kate set about introducing them to Alice but chuckled as Blake stiffened and fixed his hair at the very sight of Alice.

John made every effort to make Alice feel welcome and enjoyed hearing stories from their yesteryears. He was keen to hear her thoughts on the bunkhouse and asked her about her life in New York. Blake, on the other hand, stayed unusually quiet.

The two women giggled as they drove Lucy round to the cattle sheds. Kate teased Alice about Blake and he was still unusually quiet when an excited Lucy alerted everyone to their arrival.

Calving was mostly going without a hitch but there had been a few assisted births necessary where the calves were either lying in the wrong position or the mothers had been in labour for much longer than they should have been. The ranch was a hive of sleep-deprived activity and Matthew and John had taken on extra ranch hands to help see them through the busy time. They had a small group of trusted men that they regularly employed for an extra couple of months each year, making calving season a little less stressful.

Kate could see the men were exhausted – they hadn't had much sleep in the last few weeks – so she did her best to keep Lucy out of their way. Instead she took her to what Lucy had nicknamed the nursery, where the mothers and calves were being kept, all the while making sure to keep her well away from the cows who still had to give birth.

Jake, who was in the 'nursery', was delighted to be in the thick of it with Owen and Cody. They were helping the newborn calves to balance on their shaky legs, where needed, so that they could drink their mother's milk while at the same time checking that the rest of the calves were managing to suckle and getting their all-important first few feeds.

29

It was a new day at Wester Lakes and Matthew, Blake and Owen were out on quads checking the remaining expectant mothers for any signs of labour. They were now just over halfway though calving season and, although exhausted, John and Matthew were happy with how things were going. So far, they had a good stock of healthy newborns and their mothers were recovering and nursing well.

The men were just stopping for a short break when Matthew's phone rang. It was Michael Morgan, an ex-colleague and friend from his old law firm in San Francisco.

After a brief conversation Matthew hung up. He turned and looked up to the mountains behind the ranch house.

"You alright?" Blake shouted across the noise of the cattle.

"Kate's divorce papers have just been finalised," Matthew blurted. "She's free, she's finally free."

"Go, go." Blake ushered him away. "We can cover you here for a bit."

"I'll only be an hour at the most," Matthew shouted, firing up his quad and heading back towards the cattle sheds to get his truck.

Meanwhile, Kate had kept the afternoon free to catch up on paperwork. She'd taken much of the last couple of weeks off to spend time with Alice; however, this afternoon she was leaving her in peace to pack. Alice's holiday was almost at an end and Kate had invited Maggie and Walter over for dinner and farewell drinks before she had to take her friend back to the airport in the morning.

Alice staying at the ranch had done both women the world of good; their friendship had survived years of being apart but was still as strong as ever. Kate had absolutely no intention of returning to New York, even if it was just for a visit, but she knew Alice would visit her at the ranch regularly. Alice had gotten along with everyone, joined in the friendly banter and been a real hit with Jake and Lucy. She had also been something of a hit with Blake, and although nothing had happened between them Kate wondered if that was just a matter of time!

Kate was sitting at her desk in the office when she heard Matthew's truck screeching to a halt outside her window. She watched as he ran into the house and listened as his footsteps disappeared upstairs. A few minutes later he came running back down again and into the office.

Breathlessly, he pleaded, "Can you come with me... please?"

Kate grabbed her jacket. "What on earth are you up to now?"

He took Kate's face in his hands and kissed her softly before taking her hand and running back out to the truck. He opened her door and Kate jumped in. She was still laughing as she watched him run around the truck and jump behind the wheel.

"I don't have long. I've left the guys with the cattle."

"Okay, but where are we going?"

"You'll see." He sped down the driveway and out of Wester Lakes.

Instead of turning right towards town Matthew turned left towards the mountains. The snow was now quickly receding from their peaks, and Kate looked out as the raw beauty of the mountains was emerging once again. She recognised the exit Matthew took as he left the highway. She watched him, still wondering what he was up to as he drove up through the trees to his favourite viewpoint and the bench he had taken her to when he had first asked her to come to Wester Lakes. Matthew pulled to a stop and, as he had done all those months before, he ran around the truck and opened her door. Taking her hand he led her to the bench.

"Okay, mister, what's going on?"

Matthew couldn't keep the smile from his face as he took both of Kate's hands in his. "Kate, I've just received a phone call."

She sat apprehensively, uncertain of his tone and wondering what could possibly be coming next. "Your divorce is through, Kate. You're free!"

Kate gasped. She threw her arms around his neck and held him tight, unable to speak, unable to move, unable to comprehend the sheer momentousness of his words.

"Are you okay?" he asked, pulling his head back a little so he could see the expression on her face. His voice was trembling with the same relief she felt, the same sense of freedom and an exhilarating sense of new beginnings.

She could only nod. Tears were running down her cheeks. She started to laugh. Unable to control either the tears or the laughter she nestled her head into Matthew's neck once again and held him tight.

"I love you, Mr Harrison," she whispered. "With all my heart I love you."

They held each other tight. That chapter of Kate's life was now over. Now her past was her past and the reality of the situation was starting to sink in. She pulled herself back and looked at Matthew. "I am free of him. I am completely free of him. He has gone, completely gone. He has absolutely no interest in Jake or Lucy. That's him out of our lives for good."

Matthew nodded. "It's a shame you can't lose his name too."

Kate paused for a moment. "I could always go back to my maiden name, although I don't know how that would work with the kids?"

"I don't know either," Matthew replied as he stood up.

He put his hand in his pocket and pulled out a little black velvet box. It looked old and had faded gold writing on the top which Kate couldn't quite make out. "I was thinking Kate Harrison has a good ring to it."

Kate watched as he got down on one knee and opened the box. "Kate, I can't imagine my life without you in it. You are the only person I have ever truly loved and the only person I want to spend my life with. Kate, will you marry me?"

She looked at him. To her he was perfect. She loved him with every breath in her body. His deep blue eyes were looking at her, pleading for an answer.

Leaning forward she cupped his face in her hands. "Yes! Yes, I will marry you."

The relief and delight were all too much for Matthew as he wrapped his arms around her. There had been times when he thought this day would never come but Kate's reaction had removed all traces of uncertainty and vulnerability in Matthew. He looked up at her again. "This ring was my grandmother's. My grandparents had a long, happy marriage and I thought it might be lucky for us. If you don't like it, we can get another."

Kate looked down at the three-diamond trilogy ring set in yellow gold sparkling in the little black box. To her it was perfect.

"It's beautiful, Matthew. It's part of here, it's part of you."

Matthew slid the ring onto Kate's finger, his relief evident for Kate to see. Sitting back up on the bench beside her he put his arm around her and pulled her close. They sat in silence, both appreciating the moment and feeling the relief at Kate's divorce as much as their delight at their own news. Matthew was first to break the silence. "I have another proposal."

She watched as he shuffled about on the bench nervously. What could possibly be coming next?

"I wondered how you and the kids would feel about them taking my name too?"

Kate looked at him, stunned at his suggestion. It wasn't a thought that had ever occurred to her.

Matthew continued, "Given the circumstances of your divorce and Adam's treatment towards the children, the courts can legally withdraw his parental rights. That would mean he had no say in the adoption. It would be entirely up to you and the children, but I could legally adopt them." Kate could only look at him, staring as she tried to process what he was suggesting. She knew he loved her children as if they were his own. She also knew they loved him as if he were their father. "It would take time. There would be a lot of paperwork, but I would get Michael at the San Francisco office to handle as much as possible and the courts would want to visit us here and do background checks on me. You can think about it, discuss it with the kids, and I will go with whatever decision the three of you make. I'll completely understand if you feel it's too much of a change for them."

"Adopt them? You...you want to adopt them?" Kate could barely say the words.

Matthew nodded; it was all he could do.

"Why don't you ask them?"

"What?" He was completely taken aback at her response. "Are you sure?"

"Yes. I know what my answer is and I'm pretty sure I know what theirs will be too. I think you should be the one to ask them. This is your gesture. It should come from you."

He pulled her back into him and held her tight, neither one of them wanting to let go.

A few hours later Kate and her children were sitting on the sofa in her bedroom waiting for Matthew. As soon as Matthew walked in Lucy ran up and hugged him as she always did, and Jake was full of questions about what had happened out on the ranch while he had been at school.

"Kids, we have some news," Kate announced, ushering her children back to sit on the sofa. Kate and Matthew knelt on the floor in front of them.

"Today, Matthew asked me to marry him." She paused to watch their reaction. Smiles were spreading across her children's faces and they were both looking at her intensely as they waited to hear her answer. "I said yes," she revealed, holding out her hand to show them her ring.

Jake and Lucy were ecstatic and threw their arms around both their mother and Matthew.

Kate signalled them to lower their voices. "No one else knows yet."

Jake looked up at Matthew. "We're going to be a family."

"We are already a family," Matthew replied. "But we're going to make it official."

Jake hugged his mother again before turning and hugging Matthew. Jake's unwavering trust and appreciation for Matthew had been solidified the day Adam had turned up at the ranch, and it was a trust that would never leave him.

"I also have a question for both of you. It's a big one and you don't have to answer today. You can go away and think about it for as long as you need."

Jake and Lucy watched Matthew as he nervously looked at their mother. "What is it?" Lucy prompted, her face still beaming at her mother and Matthew's news.

"When your mum marries me she will become Kate Harrison, not Kate Thomas. I was hoping, if it's okay with you two, that I could adopt you. That would mean that in the eyes of the law I would be your dad and your names would become Jake and Lucy Harrison. It's a very big decision so take your time and think about it. You don't have to answer until you are ready."

"You would be our real daddy?" Lucy asked, her tiny nose curling up as she looked at him quizzically.

Matthew nodded.

"But you are already like my real daddy," she gushed, before one of her usual smiles spread across her face. "I like Lucy Harrison."

Matthew pulled her down from the sofa onto his knee and gave her a hug. He looked back up at Jake, who had tears in his eyes.

"You okay, Jake?" Jake could only nod. "Are those happy tears or sad tears?"

Jake jumped down from the sofa and threw his arms around Matthew's neck. Matthew could hear him sobbing into his shoulder.

"Whatever you're thinking, it's okay, Jake. You can tell me how you feel. I won't be mad or angry." Matthew held him tight and waited until he was ready to speak. Kate watched on, unable to see his face; she rubbed his back trying to console him, having no idea what Jake was thinking. Eventually Jake pulled away.

"Are you okay?" Jake nodded. "It's okay to tell me how you feel. I won't get mad like your dad," he encouraged gently.

Jake wiped his eyes and looked at Matthew. "He never treated me like you do, ever. I want you to be my dad."

Matthew pulled Jake and Lucy in closer. "I love you both very much, never ever forget that."

Thirty minutes later Blake had collected Alice from the bunk-house for dinner and Maggie and Walter had arrived. Matthew had arranged for all the Wester Lakes ranch hands to be in the first sitting for dinner. The temporary ranch hands would come up afterwards, but this way they could share their news with the people they wanted to at the same time.

Matthew, who had Lucy in one arm, led Kate and Jake up to the kitchen.

"I was wondering where you all were," John said. "I was just about to send out a search party." He stopped talking when he realised they weren't sitting down.

"We have news," Matthew said, looking around the table. Everyone looked on tentatively.

Jesse called on Emma. "Emma, get over here. I don't think you're gonna want to miss this." Emma came scuttling across from the kitchen.

Kate looked at the faces sitting around the table. "My divorce came through today."

As congratulations started to flow Matthew put his hand up and silence fell across the table. "That's not all. I asked Kate to marry me this afternoon and she said yes. We're thinking maybe a fall wedding, here at the ranch."

The table began to erupt again in celebration and John started to get up from his seat.

"Wait, Dad, there's more."

"More?"

Silence spread across the table once again. Matthew looked down at Jake. "Do you want to share our other news, Jake?"

All eyes fell on Jake. He looked around at the family he had come to adore. He felt a huge connection to everyone sitting around the table and he knew he mattered just as much to each of them.

"Matthew is going to adopt Lucy and me."

The tears and celebrations lasted well into the night. John opened a couple of bottles of champagne and everyone chatted through the day's events. Maggie and Emma both sat chatting, looking like two happy and relieved mothers of the bride, while Alice was already planning her next trip to the ranch to help with the wedding plans and the all-important bridal shower. Blake paused for a moment to look at Alice, delighted that this would bring her back to the ranch sooner rather than later.

Suddenly John's voice could be heard resounding over everyone else.

"Jake, Lucy, that will make me your grandpa!"

There are many organisations throughout the world dedicated to helping those suffering from domestic violence; no matter their gender.

Below you will find a list of just some of those dedicated organisations. This list is intended to be a useful starting point. Please be aware that website addresses may vary from country to country.

The National Domestic Violence Hotline
UK – 01823 334244
US & Canada – 1 800 799 7233
Ireland – 046 902 3710
Australia – There are several hotline numbers listed under the One In Three Campaign
In other countries – Visit International Directory of Domestic Violence Agencies
Information available in 170 languages
www.nationaldomesticviolencehotline.org.uk

Women's Aid
www.womensaid.org.uk

Refuge
www.refuge.org.uk

Victim Support
www.victimsupport.org.uk

Samaritans
www.samaritans.org.uk

US Department of Health and Human Services
(Family and Youth Services Bureau)
www.acf.hhs.gov/fysb

Men's Advice Line
www.mensadviceline.org.uk

Mankind Initiative
www.new.mankind.org.uk

National Centre for Domestic Violence
www.ncdv.org.uk

Action on Elder Abuse
www.elderabuse.org.uk

Amnesty International
www.amnesty.org

World Health Organisation
www.who.int

Lightning Source UK Ltd.
Milton Keynes UK
UKHW040822210819
348226UK00002B/33/P

9 781781 329153